W9-ANR-810

THE GLENCOE LITERATURE LIBRARY

One Day in the Life of Ivan Denisovich

and Related Readings

Glencoe
McGraw-Hill

New York, New York   Columbus, Ohio   Woodland Hills, California   Peoria, Illinois

Acknowledgments

Grateful acknowledgment is given authors, publishers, photographers, museums, and agents for permission to reprint the following copyrighted material. Every effort has been made to determine copyright owners. In case of any omissions, the Publisher will be pleased to make suitable acknowledgments in future editions.

ONE DAY IN THE LIFE OF IVAN DENISOVICH by Aleksandr Solzhenitsyn, translated by H. T. Willetts. Translation copyright © 1992 by Farrar, Straus & Giroux and William Collins Sons & Co., Ltd. All rights reserved. Published by arrangement with Farrar, Straus & Giroux, Inc.

"Teach Your Children" by Irina Eremia Bragin from THE WASHINGTON POST MAGAZINE, January 7, 1996, pp. 15–20.

"The First Gulag Returns to Its Monastic Roots" by Margaret Shapiro. Copyright © 1994 *The Washington Post.*

From RUSSIAN TALES AND LEGENDS retold by Charles Downing, 1956, Oxford University Press.

"Requiem" by Anna Akhmatova from TWENTIETH-CENTURY RUSSIAN POETRY, edited by John Glad and Daniel Weissbort, Copyright © 1992 University of Iowa Press. Reprinted by permission of University of Iowa Press.

"Bringing the First Amendment (Live!) into the Schools" from FREE SPEECH FOR ME— BUT NOT FOR THEE by Nat Hentoff. Copyright © 1991 by Common Sense, Inc. Reprinted by permission of HarperCollins Publishers, Inc.

Cover Art: Sotheby's Picture Library

Glencoe/McGraw-Hill

A Division of The McGraw·Hill Companies

Copyright © 2000 The McGraw-Hill Companies, Inc. All rights reserved. Except as permitted under the United States Copyright Act of 1976, no part of this publication may be reproduced or distributed in any form or by any means, or stored in a database or retrieval system, without prior written permission of the publisher.

Send all inquiries to:
Glencoe/McGraw-Hill
8787 Orion Place
Columbus, OH 43240

ISBN 0-07-820376-7
Printed in the United States of America
2 3 4 5 6 7 8 9 026 04 03 02 01 00

Contents

One Day in the Life of Ivan Denisovich

Aleksandr Solzhenitsyn

THE HAMMER BANGED REVEILLE on the rail outside camp HQ at five o'clock as always. Time to get up. The ragged noise was muffled by ice two fingers thick on the windows and soon died away. Too cold for the warder to go on hammering.

The jangling stopped. Outside, it was still as dark as when Shukhov had gotten up in the night to use the latrine bucket—pitch-black, except for three yellow lights visible from the window, two in the perimeter, one inside the camp.

For some reason they were slow unlocking the hut, and he couldn't hear the usual sound of the orderlies mounting the latrine bucket on poles to carry it out.

Shukhov never overslept. He was always up at the call. That way he had an hour and a half all to himself before work parade—time for a man who knew his way around to earn a bit on the side. He could stitch covers for somebody's mittens from a piece of old lining. Take some rich foreman his felt boots while he was still in his bunk (save him hopping around barefoot, fishing them out of the heap after drying). Rush round the storerooms looking for odd jobs—sweeping up or running errands. Go to the mess to stack bowls and carry them to the washers-up. You'd get something to eat, but there were too many volunteers, swarms of them. And the worst of it was that if there was anything left in a bowl, you couldn't help licking it. Shukhov never for a moment forgot what his first foreman, Kuzyomin, had told him. An old camp wolf, twelve years inside by 1943. One day around the campfire in a forest clearing he told the reinforcements fresh from the front, "It's the law of the taiga here, men. But a man *can* live here, just like anywhere else. Know who croaks first? The guy who licks out bowls, puts his faith in the sick bay, or squeals to godfather."[1]

He was stretching it a bit there, of course. A stoolie will always get by, whoever else bleeds for him.

Shukhov always got up at once. Not today, though. Hadn't felt right since the night before—had the shivers, and some sort of ache. And hadn't gotten really warm all night. In his sleep he kept fancying he was seriously ill, then feeling a bit better. Kept hoping morning would never come.

---

1. **godfather** Soviet camp slang for political officer in charge of the network of informers.

But it arrived on time.

Some hope of getting warm with a thick scab of ice on the windows, and white cobwebs of hoarfrost where the walls of the huge hut met the ceiling.

Shukhov still didn't get up. He lay up top on a four-man bunk, with his blanket and jacket over his head, and both feet squeezed into one turned-in sleeve of his quilted jerkin. He couldn't see anything but he knew from the sounds just what was going on in the hut and in his own gang's corner. He heard the orderlies trudging heavily down the corridor with the tub that held eight pails of slops. Light work for the unfit, they call it, but just try getting the thing out without spilling it! And that bump means Gang 75's felt boots are back from the drying room. And here come ours—today's our turn to get our boots dried out. The foreman and his deputy pulled their boots on in silence except for the bunk creaking under them. Now the deputy would be off to the bread-cutting room, and the foreman to see the work assigners at HQ.

He did that every day, but today was different, Shukhov remembered. A fateful day for Gang 104: would they or wouldn't they be shunted from the workshops they'd been building to a new site, the so-called Sotsgorodok.[2] This Sotsgorodok was a bare field knee-deep in snow, and for a start you'd be digging holes, knocking in fence posts, and stringing barbed wire around them to stop yourself running away. After that—get building.

You could count on a month with nowhere to go for a warm, not so much as a dog kennel. You wouldn't even be able to light a fire out in the open—where would the fuel come from? Your only hope would be to dig, dig, dig, for all you were worth.

The foreman went off to try and fix it, looking worried. Maybe he can get some gang a bit slower off the mark dumped out there? You could never do a deal empty-handed, of course. Have to slip the senior work assigner half a kilo of fatback. Maybe a kilo, even.

Might as well give it a try—wander over to sick bay and wangle a day off. Every bone in his body was aching.

Ah, but who's warder on duty today?

Oh, yes. It's Ivan-and-a-half, the thin, lanky sergeant with black eyes. First time you saw him you were terrified, but when you got to know him he was the easiest of the lot—never put you in the hole, never dragged you off to the disciplinary officer. So lie in a bit longer, till it's time for Hut 9 to go to the mess.

The bunk swayed and trembled. Two men getting up at once. Shukhov's neighbor up top, Alyoshka the Baptist, and ex-Captain (second rank) Buynovsky.

---

2. **Sotsgorodok** Socialist settlement.

The orderlies, oldish men, had carried out both night buckets and were now wrangling over who should fetch the hot water. They bickered like shrewish women. The welder for Gang 20 slung a boot and barked at them: "If you two deadbeats don't shut up, I'll do it for you."

The boot hit a post with a thud, and the old men fell silent.

The deputy foreman of the gang next to them gave a low growl. "Vasily Fyodorich! Those rats in the food store have really screwed us this time. It was four nine-hundreds, now it's only three. Who's got to go short?"

He said it quietly, but the whole gang heard and held its breath. Somebody would find a slice missing that evening.

Shukhov just lay there on the tight-packed sawdust in his mattress. Wish it would make up its mind: either a raging fever or an end to these aches and pains. This is neither one thing nor the other.

While the Baptist was still whispering his prayers, Buynovsky came back from the latrine and joyfully brought the bad news to no one in particular.

"Hang in there, shipmates! It's a good thirty below!"

That did it. Shukhov made up his mind to go to sick bay.

But at that very moment the hand of authority whipped his jerkin and his blanket away. Shukhov threw off the jacket that covered his face and raised himself on one elbow. Down below, with his head on the level of the upper bunk, stood the gaunt Tartar.

Must have come on duty out of turn and sneaked up quietly.

"Shcha-854," the Tartar read out from the white patch on the back of the black jacket.[3] "Three days in the hole, normal working hours."

His unmistakable strangled voice could be heard all over the half-dark hut—not all the light bulbs were burning—where two hundred men slept on fifty bug-ridden bunks. All those who had not yet risen suddenly came to life and began dressing in a hurry.

"What for, citizen warder?"[4] Shukhov asked, with more self-pity in his voice than he really felt.

Normal working hours was only half punishment. You got warm food, and there was no time for brooding. Full punishment was when you weren't taken out to work.

"Didn't get up at the signal, did you? Report to HQ fast." He gave his explanation in a lazy drawl because he and Shukhov and everybody else knew perfectly well what the punishment was for.

The Tartar's hairless, crumpled face was blank. He turned around to look for victims, but whether they were in half darkness or under a light bulb, on lower or upper bed shelves, all of them were stuffing their legs into black

---

3. Prisoners were identified by a number preceded by a letter of the Cyrillic alphabet.
4. Prisoners were forbidden to use the term "comrade."

padded trousers with number patches on the left knee, or, already dressed, were buttoning themselves up and hurrying toward the door to wait for the Tartar outside.

If Shukhov had done something to deserve it, he wouldn't have minded so much. What upset him was that he was always one of the first up. But it was no good asking the Tartar to let him off, he knew that. He went on begging, for form's sake, standing there in the padded trousers he'd kept on all night (they had a shabby, greasy patch of their own stitched on above the left knee, with the number Shcha-854 traced on it in faded black ink), put on his jerkin (it had two similar numbers on it—one on the chest, one on the back), picked his boots out of the pile on the floor, put on his hat (with another such numbered rag on the front), and followed the Tartar outside.

All the men in Gang 104 saw Shukhov being led out, but nobody said a word: what good would it do, whatever you said? The foreman might have put in a word for him, but he wasn't there. Shukhov himself said nothing to anybody—he didn't want to irritate the Tartar. His messmates would have the sense to save his breakfast.

They went out together.

The mist in the frosty air took your breath away. Two big searchlights from watchtowers in opposite corners crossed beams as they swept the compound. Lights were burning around the periphery, and inside the camp, dotted around in such numbers that they made the stars look dim.

The snow squeaked under the boots of the zeks[5] hurrying about their business—to the latrine, to the storeroom, to the parcel room, to hand in meal they wanted cooked separately. Heads were drawn well down into shoulders, jackets buttoned tight. Their owners were chilled not so much by the frost as by the thought that they would be outside all day in it.

The Tartar marched steadily on in his old greatcoat with grubby blue shoulder tabs. The frost didn't seem to trouble him.

They walked by the high board fence around the BUR (the camp's stone punishment cell), past the barbed-wire fence that protected the camp bakery from the prisoners, past the corner of the staff hut where a frosted length of rail dangled at the end of a thick wire, past the frost-covered thermometer hanging on another post, in a sheltered spot so that it would not fall too low. Shukhov squinted hopefully at the milk-white tube; if it showed forty-one below, they weren't supposed to be marched out to work. But it was nowhere near forty today.

They went into the HQ hut and straight through to the warders' room. It was just as Shukhov had guessed on the way. He wasn't bound for the hole—it was just that the floor of the warders' room needed washing. The

---

5. **zeks** Prison-camp slang for convicts.

Tartar announced that he forgave Shukhov and ordered him to clean it.

Washing the floor was a job for the hut orderly, a zek who wasn't sent out to work. But he had made himself so much at home in the HQ hut that he had access to the offices of the major, the disciplinary officer, and the godfather, made himself useful to them, heard a few things even the warders did not know, so for some time now he'd regarded cleaning floors for mere warders as demeaning. They'd sent for him a time or two, then realized how things stood and started "pulling" one or another of the working prisoners to clean the floor.

The heat from the stove in the warders' room was fierce. Two warders, stripped down to their dirty tunics, were playing checkers, and a third, still wearing his tightly belted sheepskin coat and felt boots, was asleep on a narrow bench.

Shukhov happily thanked the Tartar for forgiving him. "Thank you, citizen warder! I'll never sleep in again."

The rule was simple: Leave as soon as you finish. Now that Shukhov had a job to do, his body seemed to have stopped aching. He took the bucket, and just as he was, without mittens (he'd left them under the pillow in the rush), went out to the well.

Several of the foremen reporting to the PPS[6] had crowded around the post, and one, a youngish man, ex-Hero of the Soviet Union, had shinned up and was rubbing the frost off the thermometer.

Advice reached him from down below.

"Don't breathe on it, man, or it'll go up."

"Go up? In a pig's ear. That doesn't make any difference."

Shukhov's foreman, Tyurin, was not among them. He put his bucket down, worked his hands into opposite sleeves, and watched curiously.

The man up the pole said hoarsely: "Twenty-seven and a half below . . ."

He looked harder to make sure, and jumped down.

"Bullshit. It doesn't work properly," somebody said. "Think they'd hang it where we can see it if it did?"

The foremen went their ways and Shukhov trotted to the well. His earflaps were down but not tied under his chin and the frost made his ears ache.

There was such thick ice around the wellhead that the bucket would hardly go into the hole. The rope was as stiff as a pole.

When he got back to the warders' quarters with his steaming bucket, there was no feeling in his hands. He plunged them into the well water and felt a little warmer.

---

6. **PPS** Production Planning Section.

The Tartar was missing, but four others had gathered. Checkers and sleep had been forgotten, and they were discussing how much millet they would be given in January. (There was a shortage of foodstuff in the settlement, but the warders were able to buy extra supplies at discount prices, although they had long ago used up their ration coupons.)

One of them broke off to yell at Shukhov. "Pull the door to, you shit! There's a draft here!"

Wouldn't be a good idea at all to start the day with his boots wet, and he had no others to change into, even if he could dash over to the hut. Shukhov had seen all sorts of arrangements about footwear during his eight years inside: you might walk around all winter without felt boots, you might never even see a pair of ordinary shoes, just birch-bark clogs or the Chelyabinsk Tractor Factory type—strips off old tires that left tread marks in the snow. But things seemed to have improved lately. Last October he'd tagged along to the clothing store with the deputy foreman and got hold of a pair of stout shoes with hard toe caps and room for two warm foot rags in each. He'd walked around for a whole week as though it was his birthday, making a clatter with his new heels. Then, in December, felt boots had turned up as well: life was a bed of roses, no need to die just yet. So some fiend in the accounts office had whispered in the big man's ear: let them have the felt boots, but only if they hand their shoes in: it's against the rules for a zek to have two pairs at once. So Shukhov had faced a choice: either wear shoes all winter or turn them in and wear felt boots even when it thawed. He'd taken such good care of his nice new shoes, he'd greased them to make them soft . . . He'd never missed anything so much in all those eight years. The shoes were all tossed on one big pile—no hope of getting your own pair back when spring came. It was just like the time when they rounded everybody's horses up for the kolkhoz.[7]

Shukhov knew what to do this time: he stepped nimbly out of his felt boots, stood them in a corner, tossed his foot rags after them (his spoon tinkled as it hit the floor—he'd had to get ready for the hole in a hurry, but he still hadn't forgotten his spoon)—and, barefoot, dived at the warders' felt-booted feet, generously splashing the floor around them with water from his floor cloth.

"Hey! Take it easy, you crud," one of them exclaimed, quickly drawing his feet up onto his chair.

"Rice, you say? The rice allowance is different. There's no comparison with millet."

"Why are you using all that water, you idiot? What a way to wash a floor!"

---

7. **kolkhoz** Reference to the process of forcible collectivization in the early 1930s.

"Never get it clean any other way, citizen warder. The dirt's eaten into the floor."

"Did you never see your old woman clean a floor, you moron?"

Shukhov straightened up, holding the dripping floor cloth. He smiled innocently, showing the gaps left in his teeth by an attack of scurvy he had when he was on his last legs at Ust-Izhma in '43. He'd thought he was done for—a bleeding diarrhea had drained all the strength out of him and he couldn't keep anything in his stomach. Now he only had a slight lisp to remind him of it all.

"They parted my old woman and me in '41, citizen officer. I don't even remember what she looks like."

"That's what they call cleaning a floor. The bastards can't do any damned thing properly, and they don't want to learn. They aren't worth the bread we give them. Feed them on shit, I would."

"Why the hell does it have to be washed every day, anyway? It never has time to get dry. Listen here, 854! Just give it a once-over, don't make it too wet, and get the hell out of here!"

"Rice, man! There's no way you can compare it with millet!"

Shukhov made a quick job of it.

There are two ends to a stick, and there's more than one way of working. If it's for human beings—make sure and do it properly. If it's for the big man—just make it look good.

Any other way, we'd all have turned our toes up long ago, that's for sure.

Shukhov wiped the floorboards, leaving no dry patches, and without stopping to wring it out tossed the rag behind the stove. He pulled his boots on in the doorway, splashed the water out on the path along which the screws walked, and took a shortcut past the bathhouse, past the dark, chilly recreation center toward the mess hut.

He had to get to sick bay while there was still time—he was aching all over again. And he mustn't let the warders catch him outside the mess hut: the camp commandant had given strict orders to pick up stragglers and shove them in the hole.

Funny thing—no big crowd, no queue, outside the mess today. Walk right in.

It was like a bathhouse inside—whenever the door opened, frosty air mingled with the steam from the skilly. Some work gangs were sitting at tables, others were blocking the aisles waiting for vacant places. Two or three workers from every gang shouted and shoved their way through the mob, carrying bowls of skilly and gruel on wooden trays and looking for a space to put them down on. Must be deaf, the blockhead, take that for bumping the tray and making me spill the stuff! That's it—use your free hand—give him one in the neck. That's the stuff! You there, don't get in the way looking for leftovers.

There's a young fellow at that table over there crossing himself before he dips his spoon in. One of Bendera's lot,[8] must be. And a new boy at that. The older ones give it up when they've been inside a bit.

The Russians don't even remember which hand you cross yourself with.

It's cold sitting in the mess hut. Most men eat with their caps on, but they take their time, angling for gluey scraps of rotten little fish under the leaves of frost-blackened cabbage, and spitting the bones onto the table. When there's a mountain of them, somebody will sweep them off before the next gang sits down, and they will be crunched to powder underfoot.

Spitting bones out on the floor is considered bad manners.

There were two rows of pillars or stanchions, down the middle of the hut. Fetyukov, a workmate of Shukhov's, sat by one, looking after his breakfast for him. Fetyokov was one of the lowliest members of the gang—even Shukhov was a cut above him. Outwardly, the gang all looked the same, all wearing identical black jackets with identical number patches, but underneath there were big differences. You'd never get Buynovsky to sit watching a bowl, and there were jobs that Shukhov left to those beneath him.

Fetyukov caught sight of him and gave up his seat with a sigh. "It's all gone cold. I nearly ate it for you, I thought you were in the hole."

He didn't wait around. He knew Shukhov would polish both bowls till they shone and leave nothing for him.

Shukhov drew his spoon from his boot. That spoon was precious, it had traveled all over the north with him. He'd cast it himself from aluminum wire in a sand mold and scratched on it: "Ust-Izhma, 1944."

Next, he removed his cap from his shaven head—however cold it was, he wouldn't let himself eat with his cap on—and stirred up his skilly, quickly checking what had found its way into his bowl. Could have been worse. Not ladled from the top of the caldron, but not the dregs either. Fetyukov could have fished out the potato while he was guarding the bowl—be just like him!

The best you can ever say for skilly is that it's hot, but this time Shukhov's was cold. He started eating slowly, savoring it, just the same. If the roof burst into flames, he still wouldn't hurry. Apart from sleep, an old lag can call his life his own only for ten minutes at breakfast time, five at lunchtime, and five more at suppertime.

The skilly didn't change from day to day. What was in it depended on which vegetable was stockpiled for winter. Last year they'd laid in nothing but carrots in brine—so from September to June it was carrots all the way. This time around, it was black cabbage. June is when the zek eats best: the vegetables run out, and there's meal instead. The leanest time is July, when chopped nettles go into the pot.

---

8. A member of the Ukrainian nationalist underground.

There was nothing much left of the little fish, only bones: the flesh had come away and dissolved, except for scraps of head and tail. Shukhov left neither flesh nor scales on the brittle skeletons. He chomped and sucked them between his lips, then spat them out on the table. He ate every bit of every fish, gills, tails, even eyes if they were where they should be, but if they had boiled out of the head and were floating loose in the bowl—big fish eyes goggling at him—he wouldn't eat them. The others laughed at him for it.

He'd been thrifty today. He hadn't gone to the hut for his ration and was eating without bread. He could wolf it down by itself later on. More filling that way.

The second course was *magara* gruel. It had congealed into a solid bar. Shukhov broke bits off. *Magara* is bad enough hot—tastes of nothing, leaves you feeling empty. Yellowish like millet, but just grass, really. Somebody's bright idea, serving it instead of meal. Seemed they got it from the Chinese. Maybe three hundred grams, boiled weight. So make the best of it: call it what you like, it was all you were getting.

Shukhov licked his spoon clean and returned it to his boot, then put on his cap and made for sick bay.

The camp lights had chased the stars from the sky, and it was as dark as before. The broad beams from the corner towers were still quartering the compound. When they first set up this "special" camp,[9] the guards still had stacks of army surplus flares, and as soon as the light faded they would fill the air over the camp with white, green, and red fires. It was like a battlefield. Then they stopped throwing the things around. Probably cost too much.

It was just as dark as at reveille, but an experienced eye could tell from all sorts of little signs that the signal for works parade would soon be sounded. Limpy's assistant (Limpy, the mess orderly, was able to keep and feed a helper) went to call Hut No. 6—those too unfit to leave the compound—to breakfast. The old artist with the little beard ambled off to the Culture and Education Department for brush and ink to paint numbers. Yet again the Tartar strode rapidly across the midway toward the staff hut. The people had suddenly thinned out on the ground—they were all skulking inside, warming themselves in the few sweet minutes left.

Shukhov ducked around the corner of a hut: if the Tartar spotted him, he'd give him hell again. You had to be wide awake all the time. Make sure a warder never saw you on your own, only as one of a crowd. He might be looking for somebody to do a job, or he might just want to take his spite out on you. They'd gone around every hut reading out the order: prisoners must

---

9. These hard-labor prison camps, established in the late 1940s, were intended specifically for prisoners accused of political crimes under Article 58 of the Criminal Code.

take off their caps when they see a warder five paces away, and keep them off till they are two paces past him. Some warders wandered by blindly, but others made a meal of it. The hellhounds had hauled any number off to the cooler because of the "caps off" order. Better wait around the corner for a while.

The Tartar went past, and Shukhov had made up his mind to go to sick bay, when it suddenly dawned on him that he had arranged with the lanky Latvian in Hut 7 to buy two tumblers full of homegrown tobacco that morning. With so much to do, it had gone clean out of his mind. The lanky Latvian had been given his parcel the night before, and by tomorrow there might be no tobacco left. It would be a month before he got another, and it was good stuff, just strong enough and sweet-smelling. A sort of reddish-brown, it was.

Vexed with himself, Shukhov almost turned on his heel and went back to Hut 7. But sick bay was quite close and he made for its porch at a trot.

The snow squeaked under his feet.

It was always so clean in sick bay that you were afraid to tread on the floor. The walls were bright with white enamel paint, and all the fittings were white.

But the doctors' doors were all shut. Not out of bed yet, you could bet. The medical orderly on duty, a young fellow called Kolya Vdovushkin, was sitting in a crisp white gown at a clean desk, writing.

There was nobody else around.

Shukhov took off his cap as though to a superior officer. He had the old lag's habit of letting his eyes wander where they shouldn't, and he noticed that Kolya was writing lines of exactly the same length, leaving a margin and starting each one with a capital letter exactly below the beginning of the last. He knew right off, of course, that this wasn't work but something on the side. None of his business, though.

"It's like this, Nikolai Semyonich, I feel sort of poorly." There was embarrassment in his voice, as though he was asking for something that wasn't rightfully his.

Vdovushkin raised large mild eyes from his work. He was wearing a white cap, and white overalls with no number patches.

"Why so late? Why didn't you come last night? Don't you know there's no clinic in the morning? The sick list has gone over to PPS already."

Shukhov knew all that. He also knew that it was no easier to get off work in the evening.

"Yes, but, Kolya, it didn't start hurting last night, when it ought to have."

"What didn't? Where's the pain?"

"Well, when I try to put my finger on it, I can't say where it is. I just feel poorly all over."

Shukhov wasn't one of those who haunted sick bay, and Vdovushkin knew it. But he was authorized to let off only two men in the morning. And there were already two names under the greenish glass on top of the desk. With a line drawn under them.

"Well, you should have started worrying about it earlier. What's the good of coming right before work parade? Here!"

A number of thermometers had been inserted into a jar through a slit in its gauze cover. Vdovushkin drew one of them out, wiped off the solution, and gave it to Shukhov.

Shukhov sat on the very edge of a bench by the wall, just far enough not to tip over with it. He had chosen this uncomfortable place unconsciously, intending to show that he wasn't at home in sick bay and would make no great demands on it.

Vdovushkin went on writing.

The sick bay was in the most out-of-the-way corner of the camp, and no sound whatsoever reached it: there was not even the ticking of a clock—prisoners are not allowed clocks. The big boys tell the time for them. You couldn't even hear mice scratching—they'd all been caught by the hospital cat, as was his duty.

Shukhov felt strange sitting under a bright light doing nothing for five whole minutes in such deep silence in such a clean room. He inspected the walls and found nothing there. He inspected his jerkin—the number on his breast had been almost rubbed away, he'd have to get it touched up before they pounced on him. With his free hand he felt his face—his beard had come on fast in the last ten days. So what, it wasn't in his way. It would be bath day again in three days' time and he'd get a shave then. Why waste time waiting your turn at the barber's? He had nobody to make himself pretty for.

Looking at Vdovushkin's snow-white cap, Shukhov remembered the field hospital on the River Lovat—he'd gone there with a damaged jaw, and gone back into the line of his own free will, stupid clod, when he could have had five days' rest.

His one dream now was to fall sick for two or three weeks. Not fatally, of course, and he didn't want an operation. Just sick enough to be put in the hospital. He could see himself lying there for three weeks without stirring, being fed on clear beef broth. Suit him nicely, that would.

Only now, he remembered, there was no way of getting any rest. A new doctor, Stepan Grigorich, had arrived with one of the recent batches. He was fast and furious, always on the boil himself, and he made sure the patients got no peace. One of his bright ideas was turning out the patients who could walk to work in the hospital precincts—putting up fences, laying paths, shoveling extra soil onto flower beds, and—in the winter—banking snow to keep the ground warm. Work, he reckoned, was the best medicine of all.

Work is what horses die of. Everybody should know that. If he ever had to bust a gut bricklaying, he'd soon quiet down.

. . . Meanwhile, Vdovushkin went on with his writing. It was, in fact, "something on the side," but nothing that Shukhov would have comprehended. He was copying out his long new poem. He had put the finishing touches to it the night before and had promised to show it to the new doctor, Stepan Grigorich, that morning.

It was the sort of thing that happens only in camp: Stepan Grigorich had advised Vdovushkin to call himself a medical orderly and had given him the job. Vdovushkin was now practicing intravenous injections on ignorant prisoners and meek Lithuanians and Estonians, to whom it would never occur that a medical orderly could be nothing of the kind, but a former student of literature, arrested in his second year of university. Stepan Grigorich wanted him to write in prison what he hadn't had a chance to write outside.

. . . The signal for work parade could barely be heard through double windows shuttered by white ice. Shukhov sighed and stood up. He still felt feverish, but he could see that he wasn't going to get away with it. Vdovushkin reached for the thermometer and looked at it.

"There you are––neither one thing nor the other. Thirty-seven point two. If it was thirty-eight,[10] nobody would argue. I can't let you off, but you can stay if you feel like risking it. The doctor will look you over and let you off if he thinks you're ill, but if he reckons you're fit, you'll be in the hole for malingering. I'd go to work if I were you."

Shukhov rammed on his hat and left without a word or a nod.

Can a man who's warm understand one who's freezing?

The frost was cruel. A stinging haze wrapped around him and set him coughing. The air temperature was twenty-seven below and Shukhov's temperature was thirty-seven above. No holds barred!

He trotted to the hut. The midway was empty right across. The whole camp looked empty. It was that last, short, painfully sweet moment when there was no escape but everybody still pretended that work parade would never come. The guards would still be sitting in their warm barracks, resting their sleepy heads on their rifle butts. Teetering on watchtowers in such a hard frost was no fun either. The sentries in the main guardhouse would be shoveling more coal into the stove. The warders would be smoking one last cigarette before the body search. And the zeks, dressed up in all their rags and tatters, girded with lengths of rope, muffled from chin to eyes in face rags to keep the frost out, would be lying boots and all on top of their blankets, eyes shut, lost to the world. Waiting for the foreman to yell, "We're off!"

---

10. 37.2° Celsius equals 99° Fahrenheit; 38°C equals 100.4°F.

Gang 104 dozed with the rest of Hut 9. Except for Pavlo, the deputy foreman, who was moving his lips as he added up something with a pencil, and Alyoshka, the well-washed Baptist, Shukhov's neighbor, who was reading the notebook into which he had copied half the New Testament.

Shukhov dashed in but without too much noise and went over to the deputy foreman's bed.

Pavlo raised him head. "Didn't land in the hole, then, Ivan Denisovich? Still among the living?" (Western Ukrainians never learn. Even in the camps they speak to people politely.)

He picked up Shukhov's portion of bread from the table and held it out. A little hillock of sugar had been scooped onto it.

Shukhov was in a great hurry, but still thanked him properly. (The deputy foreman was one of his bosses, and more important to Shukhov than the camp commandant.) Nor was he in too much of a hurry to dip his lips in the sugar and lick them, as he hoisted himself up with one foot on the bed bracket to straighten his bedding, or to view his bread ration from all angles and weigh it on his hand in mid-air, wondering whether it contained the regulation five hundred and fifty grams. Shukhov had drawn a few thousand bread rations in jails and prison camps, and though he'd never had the chance to weigh his portion on the scales, and anyway was too timid to kick up a fuss and demand his rights, he knew better than most prisoners that a bread cutter who gave full measure wouldn't last long at the job. Every portion was underweight—the only question was by how much. Twice a day you looked at it and tried to set your mind at rest. Maybe they haven't robbed me blind this time? Maybe it's only a couple of grams short?

About twenty grams light, Shukhov decided, and broke the bread in two. He shoved one half into a little white pocket stitched inside his jerkin (prison jerkins come from the factory without pockets). The other half, saved from breakfast, he thought of eating there and then, but food swallowed in a hurry is food wasted, you feel no fuller and it does nothing for you. He made as if to stow the half ration in his locker, but changed his mind when he remembered that the hut orderlies had been beaten up twice for stealing. A big hut is about as safe as an open yard.

So, without letting go of the bread, Ivan Denisovich slipped out of his boots, deftly leaving spoon and foot rags in place, scrambled barefoot onto the top bunk, widened the hole in his mattress, and hid his half ration amid the sawdust. Then he tugged off his cap and unsheathed a threaded needle— also well hidden. (They'd feel your cap during the body search. A warder had once pricked himself and nearly smashed Shukhov's skull in his rage.) Stitch, stitch, stitch and he'd tacked up the hole over the hidden half ration. By then the sugar had melted in his mouth. Every fiber in his body was tensed to the utmost: the work assigner would be bellowing at the door any moment now. His fingers were wonderfully nimble, and his mind raced ahead, planning his next moves.

The Baptist was reading his Bible, not altogether silently, but sort of sighing out the words. This was meant perhaps for Shukhov. (A bit like political agitators, these Baptists. Loved spreading the word.)

"But let none of you suffer as a murderer, or a thief, or a wrongdoer, or a mischief-maker; yet if one suffers as a Christian, let him not be ashamed, but under that name let him glorify God."[11]

Alyoshka was a champion at one thing: wiggling that little book of his into a crack in the wall so neatly that it had never been found by searching warders.

With the same rapid movements, Shukhov draped his overcoat over the end of his bed, pulled his mittens out from under the mattress, together with another pair of flimsy foot rags, a rope, and a rag with two tapes attached to it. He did a lovely job of smoothing down the bumps in the mattress (the sawdust was heavy and close-packed), tucked the blanket under all around, tossed the pillow into place, and, still barefoot, lowered himself and began putting on his boots—first, though, the good, new foot rags, with the worn ones over them.

That was when the foreman stood up and barked: "Rise and shine, 104! Let's have you outside!"

Every man in the gang, nodding or not, rose to his feet, yawned, and made for the door. After nineteen years inside, the foreman wouldn't hustle his men out a minute too early. When he said "Out," you knew there was nothing else for it.

While the men tramped wordlessly one after another into the corridor, then through the entryway out onto the porch, and the foreman of No. 20, taking his cue from Tyurin, called "All out" in turn, Shukhov had managed to pull his boots over the two layers of foot rags, put his overcoat on over his jerkin, and tie a length of rope tightly around his waist. (If you arrived in a special camp with a leather belt, it was taken away from you—not allowed.)

So he was ready on time, and caught up with the last of his gang as their numbered backs were passing through the door onto the porch. In single file, making no effort to keep up with each other, every man looking bulky because he was muffled up in every piece of clothing he possessed, they trudged across to the midway with not a sound except for the crunch of snow underfoot.

It was still dark, although a greenish light was brightening in the east. A thin, treacherous breeze was creeping in from the same direction.

There is no worse moment than when you turn out for work parade in

---

11. I Peter 4:15–16.

the morning. In the dark, in the freezing cold, with a hungry belly, and the whole day ahead of you. You lose the power of speech. You haven't the slightest desire to talk to each other.

The junior work assigner was restlessly pacing the midway. "Come on, Tyurin, how long have we got to wait for you? Dragging your feet again, eh?"

Somebody like Shukhov might be afraid of the junior work assigner, but Tyurin wasn't. Wouldn't waste breath on him in that frost. Just tramped ahead without a word. And the whole gang tramped after him: stomp, stomp, crunch, crunch.

Tyurin must have handed over the kilo of fatback, though—because, looking at the other teams, you could see that 104 was in its old position. Some other lot, poorer and more stupid, would be shunted off to Sotsgorodok. It would be murder out there—twenty-seven below, with a mean wind blowing, no shelter, and no hope of a warm!

The foreman needed plenty of fatback—for the PPS, and to keep his own belly purring. He might not get parcels himself, but he never went short. Every man in the gang who did get a parcel gave him a present right away.

It was that or perish.

The senior work assigner was ticking off names on his board.

"One sick, Tyurin, twenty-three on parade?"

The foreman nodded. "Twenty-three."

Who was missing? Panteleyev. Who said he was sick, though?

A whisper went around the gang. Panteleyev, that son of a bitch, had stayed behind in camp again. He wasn't sick at all, the security officer had kept him back. He'd be squealing on somebody again.

Nothing to stop them sending for him later in the day and keeping him for three hours if necessary. Nobody would be there to see or hear.

They could pretend he was in sick bay.

The whole midway was black with prison jackets as the gangs slowly jostled each other toward the checkpoint. Shukhov remembered that he'd meant to freshen up the number on his jerkin, and squeezed through the crowd to the other side of the road. Two or three zeks were lining up for the artist already. Shukhov stood behind them. Those numbers were the plague of a zek's life. A warder could spot him a long way off. One of the guards might make a note of it. And if you didn't get it touched up in time, you were in the hole for not looking after it!

There were three artists in the camp. They painted pictures for the bosses, free, and also took turns painting numbers on work parade. This time it was the old man with the little gray beard. The way his brush moved as he painted a number on a cap made you think of a priest anointing a man's forehead with holy oil. He would paint for a bit and then stop to breathe into his glove. It was a thin knitted glove, and his hand would get too numb to trace the figures.

The artist renewed the Shcha-854 on Shukhov's jerkin. He wasn't far from the search point, so he didn't bother to fasten his jacket but overtook the rest of the gang with his rope belt in his hand. He suddenly spotted a chance of scrounging a butt: one of the gang, Tsezar, was smoking a cigarette instead of his usual pipe. Shukhov didn't ask straight out, though. Just took his stand near Tsezar, half facing him and looking past him.

He was gazing at something in the distance, trying to look uninterested, but seeing the cigarette grow shorter and the red tip creep closer to the holder every time Tsezar took an absentminded drag.

That scavenger Fetyukov was there too, leeching onto Tsezar, standing right in front of him and staring hot-eyed at his mouth.

Shukhov had not a shred of tobacco left, and couldn't see himself getting hold of any before evening. He was on tenterhooks. Right then he seemed to yearn for that butt more than for freedom itself, but he wouldn't lower himself like Fetyukov, wouldn't look at Tsezar's mouth.

Tsezar was a mixture of all nationalities. No knowing whether he was Greek, Jew, or gypsy. He was still young. Used to make films, but they'd put him inside before he finished his first picture. He had a heavy black walrus mustache. They'd have shaved it off, only he was wearing it when they photographed him for the record.

Fetyukov couldn't stand it any longer. "Tsezar Markovich," he drooled. "Save me just one little drag."

. . . Tsezar raised his half-closed eyelids and turned his dark eyes on Fetyukov. He'd taken to smoking a pipe to avoid this sort of thing—people barging in, begging for the last drag. He didn't grudge them the tobacco, but he didn't like being interrupted when he was thinking. He smoked to set his mind racing in pursuit of some idea. But the moment he lit a cigarette he saw "Leave a puff for me!" in several pairs of eyes.

. . . He turned to Shukhov and said, "Here you are, Ivan Denisovich."

His thumb eased the glowing butt out of the short amber holder.

That was all Shukhov had been waiting for. He sprang into action and gratefully caught hold of the butt, keeping the other hand underneath for safety. He wasn't offended that Tsezar was too fussy to let him finish the cigarette in the holder. Some mouths are clean, others are dirty, and anyway his horny fingers could hold the glowing tip without getting burned. The great thing was that he'd cut the scavenger Fetyukov out and was now inhaling smoke, with the hot ash beginning to burn his lips. Ah, lovely. The smoke seemed to reach every part of his hungry body, he felt it in his feet as well as in his head.

But no sooner had this blissful feeling pervaded his body than Ivan Denisovich heard a rumble of protest: "They're taking our undershirts off us."

A zek's life was always the same. Shukhov was used to it: relax for a minute and somebody was at your throat.

What was this about undershirts? The camp commandant had issued them himself. No, it couldn't be right.

There were only two gangs ahead waiting to be searched, so everybody in 104 got a good view: the disciplinary officer, Lieutenant Volkovoy, walked over from HQ hut and barked at the warders. They had been frisking the men halfheartedly before Volkovoy appeared, but now they went mad, setting upon the prisoners like wild beasts, with the head warder yelling, "Unbutton your shirts!"

Volkovoy was dreaded not just by the zeks and the warders but, so it was said, by the camp commandant himself. God had marked the scoundrel with a name to suit his wolfish looks.[12] He was lanky, dark, beetle-browed, quick on his feet: he would pop up when you least expected him, shouting, "Why are you all hanging around here?" There was no hiding from him. At one time he'd carried a lash, a plaited leather thing as long as your forearm. They said he thrashed people with it in the camp jail. Or else, when zeks were huddled outside the door during the evening hut search, he would creep up and slash you across the neck with it: "Why aren't you lined up properly, you scum?" The crowd would reel back like an ebbing wave. The whipped man would clutch his burning neck, wipe the blood away, and say nothing: he didn't want a spell in the hole as well.

Just lately he'd stopped carrying his lash for some reason.

In frosty weather, body searches were usually less strict in the morning than in the evening; the prisoner simply undid his jacket and held its skirts away from his body. Prisoners advanced five at a time, and five warders stood ready for them. They slapped the sides of each zek's belted jerkin, and tapped the one permitted pocket on his right knee. They would be wearing gloves themselves, and if they felt something strange they didn't immediately pull it out but lazily asked what it was.

What would you expect to find on a zek in the morning? A knife? They don't carry knives out, they bring them in. Just make sure he hasn't got three kilograms of food on him, to run away with—that's all that matters in the morning. At one time they got so worried about the two hundred grams every zek took with him for dinner that each gang was ordered to make a wooden chest to hold the lot. Why the bastards thought that would do any good was a mystery. They were probably just out to make life more miserable, give the men something extra to worry about. You took a bite and looked hard at your bread before you put it in the chest. But the pieces were still all alike, still just bread, so you couldn't help fretting all the way to work in case somebody switched rations. Men argued with each other and sometimes came to blows. Then one day three men helped themselves to a

---

12. *Volk* means "wolf" in Russian.

chest full of bread and escaped from a work site in a truck. The brass came to their senses, had the chests chopped up in the guardhouse, and let everybody carry his own ration again.

Another thing the searchers looked for in the morning: men wearing civilian dress under prison clothes. Never mind that everybody had been stripped of his civilian belongings long ago, and told that he'd get them back the day his sentence ended (a day nobody in that camp had yet seen).

And one other thing—prisoners carrying letters for free workers to smuggle out. Only, if you searched everybody for letters, you'd be messing about till dinnertime.

But Volkovoy only had to bawl out an order and the warders peeled off their gloves, made the prisoners unbelt the jerkins under which they were all hugging the warmth of the hut and unbutton their shirts, and set about feeling for anything hidden underneath contrary to regulations. A zek was allowed two shirts—shirt and undershirt; everything else must come off. That was the order from Volkovoy relayed from rank to rank. The teams that had gone past earlier were the lucky ones. Some of them were already through the gates, but for those left behind, it was "Open up!" All those with too much on underneath must take it off right there in the cold.

They made a start, but the result was confusion: the gates had already been cleared and the guards were bawling, "Hurry it up! Let's go!" So Volkovoy swallowed his wrath and let 104 off lightly: note down those wearing anything extra, and make them turn everything in to the clothes store at the end of the day, together with an explanation in writing where and why they hid it.

Shukhov was wearing only camp issue anyway: go ahead, he told them silently, have a feel, nothing here except a bare chest with a soul inside it. But a note was made of Tsezar's flannel vest, and Buynovsky—surprise—had a little waistcoat or cummerbund of some sort. Buynovsky shouted at the top of his voice—he'd been used to torpedo boats, and had spent less than three months in the camp. "You have no right to make people undress in freezing cold! You don't know Article 9 of the Criminal Code!"

But they did have. They did know. It's you, brother, who don't know anything yet!

The captain kept blazing away at them: "You aren't real Soviet people!"

Volkovoy didn't mind Article 9, but at this he looked as black as a thundercloud.

"Ten days' strict regime!" he shouted.

"Starting this evening," he told the head warder, lowering his voice.

They never like putting a man in the hole first thing in the morning: it means the loss of one man-shift. Let him sweat and strain all day, and sling him in the hole at night.

The jailhouse stood nearby, to the left of the midway: a stone building, with two wings. The second wing had been added that autumn—there wasn't room enough in just one. It was an eighteen-cell jail and there were walled-off recesses for solitary confinement. The rest of the camp was built of wood, only the jail was of stone.

Now that the cold had been let in under their shirts, there was no getting rid of it. They had all muffled themselves up for nothing. And the dull pain in Shukhov's back would not go away. If only he could lie down there and then on a cot in sick bay and sleep. He had no other wish in the world. Just a good heavy blanket.

The zeks stood near the gate buttoning and belting themselves, with the guards outside yelling, "Hurry it up! Let's go!"

And the work assigner was also shoving them from behind and shouting, "Let's go! Look alive!"

Through the first gate. Into the outer guarded area. Through the second gate. Between the railings by the guardhouse.

"Halt!" roared the sentry. "Like a flock of sheep! Sort yourselves out in fives!"

By now the darkness was lifting. The bonfire lit by the convoy guards was burning out. They always got a good fire going before work parade—so they could keep warm and see better to count.

One of the sentries counted them off in a loud, harsh voice: "First five! Second! Third!"

And the groups of five peeled off and moved forward in separate ranks so that, looking from the front or from behind, you saw five heads, five trunks, and ten legs.

A second sentry stood by the railings opposite, silently checking the count.

A lieutenant also stood watching.

All this on behalf of the administration.

Every man was more precious than gold. A single head short behind the wire and your own head would make up for it.

The gang closed up again.

Now the escort party's sergeant was counting.

And again the groups of five detached themselves and went forward in separate ranks.

The assistant guard commander checked the count from the other side.

And a lieutenant double-checked.

All this on behalf of the convoy.

On no account must they make a mistake. Sign for one head too many and your own would make up the number.

There were escort troops all over the place. They held the Power Station column in a semicircular embrace, automatic weapons leveled, stuck right in your mug. Then there were the handlers with their gray dogs. One dog bared its teeth as though laughing at the zeks. The convoy were all wearing short fur coats, except for half a dozen in sheepskins. The whole shift shared the sheepskins—you put one on when it was your turn to go up on the watchtower.

Once again the convoy mixed the teams together and re-counted the Power Station column by fives.

"The cold is worst at sunup," the captain told the world. "It's the lowest point of nighttime temperature loss."

The captain was fond of explaining things. Ask him and he'd work out for you whether the moon would be new or old on whatever day in whichever year you liked.

The captain was going downhill while you watched. His cheeks were sunken. But he kept his spirits up.

Outside camp the frost, with that nagging little wind blowing, nipped even Shukhov's case-hardened features painfully. Realizing that it would be blowing in his face all the way to the Power Station, he decided to put his face cloth on. He and many of the others had a bit of rag with two long strings to tie on when they were marched into the wind. The zeks found that it helped. He buried his face in it up to his eyes, drew the strings around over the lobes of his ears, and tied them behind his head. Then he covered the back of his neck with the back flap of his cap and turned up his overcoat collar. Next he let down the front flap of his cap over his forehead. Seen from the front, he was nothing but eyes. He drew the rope end tight around his jacket. Everything was fine now, except that his mittens were not much good and his hands were stiff with cold already. He rubbed them together and clapped them, knowing that any minute now he would have to put them behind his back and keep them there the whole way.

The escort commander recited the convict's daily "prayer," of which they were all heartily sick:

"Your attention, prisoners! Keep strictly to your column on the march! No spreading out, no running into the column in front, no moving from rank to rank, keep your eyes straight ahead, keep your hands behind your backs and nowhere else! One step to the right or left will be considered an attempt to escape and the guards will open fire without warning! Leader—quick march!"

The two foremost guards marched off along the road. The column in front wavered, shoulders began swaying, and the guards twenty paces to the right and left of the column, at intervals of ten paces, moved along, weapons at the ready.

The snow on the road was packed tight and firm underfoot—none had fallen for a week. As they rounded the camp, the wind hit their faces from the side. Hands behind backs, heads lowered, the column moved off as if to a funeral. All you could see were the legs of the two or three men in front of you and the patch of trampled ground on which you were about to tread. From time to time a guard would yell: "Yu-40! Hands behind you! B-502! Close up!" Then the shouts became less frequent: keeping tabs wasn't easy in that cutting wind. The guards weren't allowed to tie rags around their faces, mind. Theirs wasn't much of a job, either.

When it was a bit warmer, they all talked on the march, however much they were yelled at. But today they kept their heads down, every man trying to shelter behind the man in front, thinking his own thoughts.

A convict's thoughts are no freer than he is: they come back to the same place, worry over the same thing continually. Will they poke around in my mattress and find my bread ration? Can I get off work if I report sick tonight? Will the captain be put in the hole, or won't he? How did Tsezar get his hands on his warm vest? Must have greased somebody's palm in the storeroom, what else?

Because he had eaten only cold food, and gone without his bread ration at breakfast, Shukhov felt emptier than usual. To stop his belly whining and begging for something to eat, he put the camp out of his mind and started thinking about the letter he was shortly going to write home.

The column went past a woodworking plant (built by zeks), past a housing estate (zeks again had assembled these huts, but free workers lived in them), past the new recreation center (all their own work, from the foundations to the murals—but it was the free workers who watched films there), and out onto the open steppe, walking into the wind and the reddening sunrise. Not so much as a sapling to be seen out on the steppe, nothing but bare white snow to the left or right.

In the year just beginning—1951—Shukhov was entitled to write two letters. He had posted his last in July, and got an answer in October. In Ust-Izhma the rules had been different—you could write every month if you liked. But what was there to say? Shukhov hadn't written any more often than he did now.

He had left home on 23 June 1941. That Sunday, people had come back from Mass in Polomnya and said, "It's war." The post office there had heard the news—nobody in Temgenyovo had a radio before the war. Shukhov knew from letters that nowadays there was piped radio jabbering away in every cottage.

Writing letters now was like throwing stones into a bottomless pool. They sank without trace. No point in telling the family which gang you worked in and what your foreman, Andrei Prokofyevich Tyurin, was like. Nowadays you had more to say to Kildigs, the Latvian, than to the folks at home.

They wrote twice a year as well, and there was no way in which he could understand how things were with them. So the kolkhoz had a new chairman—

well, it had a new one every year, they never kept one any longer. So the kolkhoz had been enlarged—well, they'd enlarged it before and cut it down to size again. Then there was the news that those not working the required number of days had had their private plots trimmed to fifteen-hundredths of a hectare, or sometimes right up to the very house. There was, his wife wrote, also a law that people could be tried and put in jail for not working the norm, but that law hadn't come into force for some reason.

One thing Shukhov couldn't take in at all was that, from what his wife wrote, not a single living soul had joined the kolkhoz since the war: all the young lads and girls had somehow wangled their way to town to work in a factory, or else to the peat works. Half of the men hadn't come back from the war, and those who had didn't want anything to do with the kolkhoz: they just stayed at home and did odd jobs. The only men on the farm were the foreman Zakhar Vasilievich and the carpenter Tikhon, who was eighty-four but had married not long ago and had children. The kolkhoz was kept going by the women who'd been herded into it back in 1930. When they collapsed, it would drop dead with them.

Try as he might, Shukhov couldn't understand the bit about people living at home and working on the side. He knew what it was to be a small-holder, and he knew what it was to be in a kolkhoz, but living in the village and not working in it was something he couldn't take in. Was it like when the men used to hire themselves out for seasonal work? How did they manage with the haymaking?

But his wife told him that they'd given up hiring themselves out ages ago. They didn't travel around carpentering anymore either—their part of the world was famous for its carpenters—and they'd given up making wicker baskets, there was no call for them. Instead, there was a lively new trade—dyeing carpets. A demobbed soldier had brought some stencils home, and it had become all the rage. There were more of these master dyers all the time. They weren't on anybody's payroll, they had no regular job, they just put in a month on the farm, for haymaking and harvest, and got a certificate saying that kolkhoz member so-and-so had leave of absence for personal reasons and was not in arrears. So they went all around the country, they even flew in airplanes to save their precious time, and they raked the money in by the thousand, dyeing carpets all over the place. They charged fifty rubles to make a carpet out of an old sheet that nobody wanted, and it only took about an hour to paint the pattern on. His wife's dearest hope was that when he got home he would keep clear of the kolkhoz and take up dyeing himself. That way they could get out of the poverty she was struggling against, send their children to trade schools, and build themselves a new cottage in place of their old tumble-down place. All the dyers were building themselves new houses. Down by the railroad, houses now cost twenty-five thousand instead of the five thousand they cost before.

Shukhov still had quite a bit of time to do—a winter, a summer, another winter, another summer—but all the same, those carpets preyed on his mind. It could be just the job if he was deprived of rights or banished. So he asked his wife to tell him how he could be a dyer when he'd been no good at drawing from the day he was born? And, anyway, what was so wonderful about these carpets? What was on them? She wrote back that any fool could make them. All you did was put the stencil on the cloth and rub paint through the holes. There were three sorts. There was the "Troika"—three horses in beautiful harness pulling a hussar officer—the "Stag," and one a bit like a Persian carpet. Those were the only patterns, but people all over the country jumped at the chance to buy them. Because a real carpet cost thousands of rubles, not fifty.

He wished he could get a peek at them.

In jail and in the camps Shukhov had lost the habit of scheming how he was going to feed his family from day to day or year to year. The bosses did all his thinking for him, and that somehow made life easier. But what would it be like when he got out?

He knew from what free workers said—drivers and bulldozer operators on construction sites—that the straight and narrow was barred to ordinary people, but they didn't let it get them down, they took a roundabout way and survived somehow.

Shukhov might have to do the same. It was easy money, and you couldn't miss. Besides, he'd feel pretty sore if others in the village got head of him. But still . . . in his heart of hearts Shukhov didn't want to take up carpet-making. To do that sort of thing you had to be the free-and-easy type, you had to have plenty of cheek, and know when to grease a policeman's palm. Shukhov had been knocking around for forty years, he'd lost half his teeth and was going bald, but he'd never given or taken a bribe outside and hadn't picked up the habit in the camps.

Easy money had no weight: you didn't feel you'd earned it. What you get for a song you won't have for long, the old folks used to say, and they were right. He still had a good pair of hands, hands that could turn to anything, so what was to stop him getting a proper job on the outside?

Only—would they ever let him go? Maybe they'd slap another ten on him, just for fun?

By then the column had arrived, and halted at the guardhouse outside the sprawling work site. Two guards in sheepskin coats had fallen out at one corner of the boundary fence and were trudging to their distant watchtowers. Nobody would be allowed onto the site until all the towers were manned. The escort commander made for the guardroom, with his weapon slung over his shoulder. Smoke was billowing out of the guardroom chimney: a free worker kept watch there all night to see that no one carried off planks and cement.

Looking through the wire gate, across the building site and out through the wire fence on the far side, you could see the sun rising, big and red, as though in a fog. Alyoshka, standing next to Shukhov, gazed at the sum and a smile spread from his eyes to his lips. Alyoshka's cheeks were hollow, he lived on his bare ration and never made anything on the side—what had he got to be happy about? He and the other Baptists spent their Sundays whispering to each other. Life in the camp was like water off a duck's back to them. They'd been lumbered with twenty-five years apiece just for being Baptists. Fancy thinking that would cure them!

The face cloth he'd worn on the march was wet through from his breath, and a thick crust of ice had formed where the frost had caught it. Shukhov pulled it down from his face to his neck and turned his back on the wind. The cold hadn't really got through anywhere, only his hands felt the chill in those thin mittens, and the toes of his left foot were numb, because he'd burnt a hole in his felt boot and had to patch it twice.

He couldn't see himself doing much work with shooting pains in his midriff and all the way up his back.

He turned around and found himself looking at the foreman. He'd been marching in the last rank of five. Hefty shoulders, the foreman had, and a beefy face to match. Always looked glum. Not one to share a joke with the men, but kept them pretty well fed, saw to it they got good rations. A true son of the Gulag. On his second sentence, and he knew the drill inside out.

Your foreman matters more than anything else in a prison camp: a good one gives you a new lease of life, a bad one can land you six feet under. Shukhov had known Andrei Prokofyevich Tyurin back in Ust-Izhma. He hadn't worked under him there, but when all the "traitors" had been shunted from the ordinary penal camp to hard labor, Tyurin had singled him out. Shukhov had no dealings with the camp commandant, the Production Planning Section, the site managers, or the engineers: his foreman was always in there standing up for him: a chest of steel, Tyurin had. But if he twitched an eyebrow or lifted a finger—you ran and did whatever he wanted. Cheat anybody you liked as long as you didn't cheat Tyurin, and you'd get by.

Shukhov wanted to ask the foreman whether they'd be working at the same place as yesterday or moving somewhere else, but didn't like to interrupt his lofty thoughts. Now he'd got Sotsgorodok off their backs, he'd be thinking about the rate for the job. The next five days' ration depended on it.

The foreman's face was deeply pockmarked. He didn't even squint as he stood looking into the wind. His skin was like the bark of an oak.

The men in the column were clapping their hands and stamping their feet. It was a nasty little wind. The poll-parrots must all be up on their perches by now, but the guards still wouldn't let the men in. They were overdoing the security.

At last! The guard commander came out of the guardhouse with the checker. They took their stand on opposite sides of the entrance and opened the gates.

"Sort yourselves out in fives! First five, second five."

The convicts marched off with something like a military step. Just let us in there, we'll do the rest!

Just past the guardhouse was the office shack. The site manager stood outside it, urging the foremen to get a move on. They hardly needed to be told. Der—the zek they'd made an overseer—went with them. A real bastard, that one, treated his fellow zeks worse than dogs.

It was eight o'clock, no, five past eight already (that was the power-supply train whistling), and the bosses were afraid the zeks would scatter and waste time in warming sheds. A zek's day is a long one, though, and he can find time for everything. Every man entering the compound stooped to pick up a wood chip or two. Do nicely for our stove. Then quick as a flash into their shelters.

Tyurin ordered Pavlo, the deputy foreman, to go with him into the office. Tsezar turned in there after them. Tsezar was rich, got two parcels a month, gave all the right people a handout, so he was a trusty, working in the office helping the norm setter.

The rest of Gang 104 scuttled out of sight.

A dim red sun had risen over the deserted compound: over pre-fab panels half buried in snowdrifts, over the brickwork of a building abandoned as soon as the foundations were laid, over the broken crank handle of an earthmoving machine, a jug, a heap of scrap iron. There were drains, trenches, holes everywhere. There were automobile-repair shops in open-fronted sheds, and there, on a rise, stood the Power Station, its ground floor completed, its first floor just begun.

Everybody had gone into hiding, except for the six sentries in their towers and the group buzzing outside the office. This moment was the zek's very own! The senior site manager, so they said, was always threatening to give each gang its assignment the night before, but they could never make it work. Anything they decided at night would be stood on its head by morning.

Yes—this moment was their very own! While the bosses were getting organized—snuggle up in the warm, sit there as long as you can, you'll have a chance to break your back later, no need to hurry. The best thing was to get near a stove and rewrap your foot rags (warm them a little bit first) so your feet would be warm all day. But even without a stove it was still pretty good.

Gang 104 went into the big auto-repair shop. Its windows had been installed in the autumn, and Gang 38 was working there, molding concrete slabs. Some slabs were still in the molds, some had been stood up on end, and there were piles of wire mesh lying around. The roof of the shop was high, and it had an earthen floor, so it would never be really warm, but still the big room was heated, and the bosses didn't spare the coal—not, of course, to keep the men warm, but to help the slabs set. There was even a thermometer hanging there, and if for some reason the camp didn't turn out to work on Sunday, a free worker kept the stoves going.

Gang 38, of course, was blocking the stove, drying their foot rags, and wouldn't let outsiders anywhere near it. Never mind, it's not too bad up in the corner here.

Shukhov rested the shiny seat of his quilted trousers on the edge of a wooden mold and propped himself against the wall. As he leaned back, his overcoat and jerkin tightened and he felt something hard pressing against the left side of his chest, near his heart. A corner of the crust in his inside pocket—the half of his morning ration he'd brought along for dinner. He always took that much to work and never touched it till dinnertime. But as a rule he ate the other half at breakfast, and this time he hadn't. So he hadn't really saved anything: he was dying to eat this portion right away while he was in the warm. It was five hours to dinnertime. A long haul.

The ache in his back had moved down to his legs now, and they suddenly felt weak. If only he could get up to the stove!

Shukhov placed his mittens on his knees, unbuttoned his jacket, untied his icy face cloth from around his neck, folded it a few times, and tucked it in his pocket. Then he took out the piece of bread in the white rag and, holding it under his coat so that not a crumb would be lost, began nibbling and chewing it bit by bit. He'd carried the bread under two layers of clothing, warming it with his body, so it wasn't the least bit frozen.

Since he'd been in the camps Shukhov had thought many a time of the food they used to eat in the village—whole frying pans full of potatoes, porridge by the caldron, and, in the days before the kolkhoz, great hefty lumps of meat. Milk they used to lap up till their bellies were bursting. But he knew better now that he'd been inside. He'd learned to keep his whole mind on the food he was eating. Like now he was taking tiny little nibbles of bread, softening it with his tongue, and drawing in his cheeks as he sucked it. Dry black bread it was, but like that nothing could be tastier. How much had he eaten in the last eight or nine years? Nothing. And how hard had he worked? Don't ask.

Shukhov, then, was busy with his two hundred grams, while the rest of Gang 104 made themselves comfortable at the same end of the shop.

The two Estonians sat like two brothers on a low concrete slab, sharing half a cigarette in a holder. They were both tow-haired, both lanky, both skinny, they both had long noses and big eyes. They clung together as though neither would have air enough to breathe without the other. The foreman never separated them. They shared all their food and slept up top on the same bunk. On the march, on work parade, or going to bed at night, they never stopped talking to each other, in their slow, quiet way. Yet they weren't brothers at all—they'd met for the first time in Gang 104. One of them, they explained, was a Baltic fisherman; the other had been taken off to Sweden by his parents when the Soviets were set up. When he grew up, he'd come back of his own free will, silly idiot, to finish his education in the land of his birth. He'd been pulled in the moment he arrived.

People said nationality didn't mean anything, that there were good and bad in every nation. Shukhov had seen lots of Estonians, and never came across a bad one.

There they all were, sitting on slabs, on molds, on the bare ground. Tongues were too stiff for talk in the morning, so everybody withdrew into his own thoughts and kept quiet. Fetyukov the scavenger had picked up a lot of butts (he'd even tip them out of the spittoon, he wasn't squeamish). Now he was taking them apart on his lap and sprinkling the half-burnt tobacco onto a single piece of paper. Fetyukov had three children on the outside, but when he was jailed they'd all turned their backs on him, and his wife had married somebody else, so he got no help from anywhere.

Buynovsky kept looking sideways at him, and suddenly barked: "Why do you pick up all that foul stuff? You'll get syphilis of the mouth before you know it! Chuck it out!"

The captain was used to giving orders. He talked to everybody like that.

But he had no hold over Fetyukov—he didn't get any parcels either. The scavenger gave a nasty little snigger—half his teeth were missing—and said: "Just you wait, Captain, when you've been inside eight years, you'll be doing the same yourself."

True enough, in its time the camp had seen off prouder people than Buynovsky.

"Eh? What's that?" Senka Klevshin hadn't heard properly. He thought they'd been talking about how Buynovsky got burnt on work parade that morning. "You'd have been all right if you hadn't flown off the handle," he said, shaking his head pityingly.

A quiet fellow, Senka Klevshin. One of the poor devil's eardrums had burst back in '41. Then he'd landed in a POW camp. Ran away three times. They'd caught up with him every time, and finally stuck him in Buchenwald. He'd escaped death by some miracle, and now he was serving his time quietly. Kick up a fuss, he said, and you're done for.

He was right there. Best to grin and bear it. Dig in your heels and they'll break you in two.

Alyoshka sat silent, with his face buried in his hands. Saying his prayers.

Shukhov nibbled his bread till his teeth met his fingers, but left a bit of the rounded upper crust: a piece of bread is better than any spoon for cleaning out a porridge bowl. He wrapped the crust in the white rag again till dinnertime, stuffed it into the pocket inside his jerkin, and buttoned himself up against the cold. Right—I'm ready for work as soon as they like to send me. Be nice if they hang about a bit longer, though.

Gang 38 got up and went their ways: some to the cement mixer, some to fetch water, some to collect wire mesh.

But neither Tyurin nor his deputy, Pavlo, had rejoined 104. And though the men had been sitting around for scarcely twenty minutes, and the working day (shortened in winter) would not end till six o'clock, they felt as happy as if it was nearly over. Kildigs, the plump, red-faced Latvian, sighed. "Long time since we had a blizzard! Not a single one all winter. What sort of winter is that?"

The gang all sighed for the blizzards they hadn't had.

When a blizzard blows up in those parts, the bosses are afraid to take the men out of their huts, let alone to work. You can get lost on the way from your hut to the mess hall unless you sling a rope between them. If a convict dies out in the snow, nobody gives a damn. But say he escapes. It has happened. In a blizzard the snow falls in tiny flakes, and the drifts are firm as though packed by hand. Men have walked up such drifts straddling the wire and out of camp. Not that they ever got far.

When you come to think of it, a blizzard is no use to anybody. The zeks sit under lock and key. Coal doesn't arrive on time, and the wind blows the warmth out of the hut. If no flour is delivered to the camp, there'll be no bread. And however long the blizzard blows, whether it's three days or a week, every single day is counted as a day off, and the men are turned out to work Sunday after Sunday to make up for lost time.

All the same, zeks love blizzards and pray for them. As soon as the wind freshens, they all throw their heads back and look at the sky: "Come on, let's have the stuff! Let's have the stuff, then!"

Meaning snow.

A ground wind never works itself up into a decent blizzard.

A man tried to get warm at Gang 38's stove and was shooed away.

Then Tyurin came into the shop scowling. The team knew that there was work to be done and quickly.

"Right, then." Tyurin looked around. "All here, 104?"

Without stopping to check or count, because nobody ever tried to give him the slip, he began giving each man his job. The two Estonians, together with Klevshin and Gopchik, were sent to fetch a big mixing trough from nearby and carry it to the Power Station. This was enough to tell the gang that it was being switched to that building, which had been left half finished in late autumn. Two men were sent to the tool shop, where Pavlo was drawing the necessary tools. Four were assigned to snow clearance around the

Power Station, at the entrance into the engine room itself, and on the catwalks. Another two were ordered to make a coal fire in the stove in the engine room—they'd have to pinch some boards and chop them up first. One man was to haul cement over on a sled. Two men would carry water, and two others sand. Another man would have to clear the snow away from the frozen sand and break it up with a crowbar.

This left only Shukhov and Kildigs—the most skilled men in the gang—without jobs.

The foreman called them aside, and said, "Listen, boys!" (He was no older than they were, but "boys" was a word he was always using.) "After dinner you'll be starting where Gang 6 left off last autumn, walling the second story with cinder blocks. But right now we must get the engine room warm. It's got three big windows, and your first job is to block them with something. I'll give you some men to help, you just think what you can use to board them up. We'll use the engine room for mixing, and to warm up in. If we don't get some heat into the place, we'll freeze to death like dogs. Got it?"

He looked as if he had more to say, but Gopchik, a lad of about sixteen, as pink-cheeked as a piglet, came running to fetch him, complaining that another gang wouldn't let him have the mixing trough and wanted to make a fight of it. So Tyurin shot off to deal with that.

It was hard starting a day's work in such cold, but that was all you had to do, make a start, and the rest was easy.

Shukhov and Kildigs looked at each other. They had worked as partners more than once before and the bricklayer and the carpenter respected each other's skills. Getting hold of something in the bare snow to stop up the windows wasn't going to be easy. But Kildigs said: "Listen, Vanya! I know a place over by the pre-fabs where there's a big roll of tarred paper doing nothing. I tucked it away myself. Why don't we pop over?"

Though he was a Latvian, Kildigs spoke Russian like a native—the people in the village next to his were Russians, Old Believers, and he'd learned the language as a child. He'd been in the camps only two years, but he knew what was what: you get nothing by asking. Kildigs's name was Jan, and Shukhov called *him* Vanya, too.

They decided to go for the tarred paper. But Shukhov hurried off first to pick up his trowel in the half-built wing of the auto-repair shop. It's very important to a bricklayer to have a trowel that's light and comfortable to hold. But the rule on every building site was collect all your tools in the morning and hand them all back at night. And it was a matter of luck what sort of tools you'd get next day. So Shukhov had diddled the toolmaker out of a very good trowel one day. He hid it in a different place every time, and got it out in the morning if there was bricklaying to be done. Of course, if they'd been marched off to Sotsgorodok that morning, he'd have been without a trowel again. But now he only had to shift a few pebbles and thrust his hand into the crevice—and out it came.

Shukhov and Kildigs left the auto-repair sheds and made for the pre-fabs. Their breath turned to dense steam as they walked. The sun was up now, but gave off a dull blurry light as if through fog, and to either side of the sun stood—fence posts? Shukhov drew Kildigs's attention to them with a nod, but Kildigs dismissed it with a laugh.

"Fence posts won't bother us, as long as wire isn't strung between them. That's what you've got to look out for."

Every word from Kildigs was a joke. The whole gang loved him for it. And the Latvians all over the camp had tremendous respect for him. But then, of course, Kildigs could count on a square meal, he got two parcels every month, he had color in his cheeks and didn't look like a convict at all. He could afford to see the funny side.

Huge, their work site was, a country walk from one side to the other. They bumped into some lads from Gang 82 on the way. They'd been made to dig holes again. Not very big holes were needed—fifty centimeters by fifty, and fifty deep. But the ground was stone even in summer, and it would take some tearing up now that the frost had a good hold. The pickax would glance off it, sparks would fly, but not a crumb of earth would be loosened. The poor fellows stood over there, each in his own hole, looking around now and then to find shelter. No, there was nowhere to go for warmth, and anyway they'd been forbidden to leave the spot, so they got to work with their picks again. That was all the warmth they'd be getting.

Shukhov saw a familiar face, a man from Vyatka, and offered him some advice. "Here. What you diggers ought to do is light a fire over every hole. That way the ground would thaw out."

"They won't let us." The Vyatka man sighed. "Won't give us any firewood."

"So find some yourself."

Kildigs could only spit in disgust.

"Come off it, Vanya, if the bosses had any brains, do you think they'd have people using pickaxes in weather like this?"

He added a few mumbled oaths and shut up. Nobody's very talkative when it's that cold. On and on they went till they reached the place where the pre-fab panels were buried under the snow.

Shukhov liked working with Kildigs, except for one thing—he didn't smoke, and there was never any tobacco in his parcels.

He had a sharp eye, though, Kildigs did: they helped each other to lift one board, then another, and underneath lay the roll of tarred paper.

They pulled it clear. The question now was how to carry it. It wouldn't matter if they were spotted from the watchtowers. The poll-parrots only worried about prisoners trying to run away. Inside the work area you could chop every last panel into splinters for all they cared. If a warder came by, that wouldn't matter either: he'd be looking around for anything he could pick up himself. And no working convict gave a damn for those pre-fabs. Nor did the foremen. Only the site manager, a free employee, the zek supervisor, and that gangling Shkuropatenko cared about them. Shkuropatenko was a nobody, just a zek, but he had the soul of a screw. He'd been put on a daily wage just to guard the pre-fabs and see that the zeks didn't make off with bits of them. Shkuropatenko was the one most likely to catch them out in the open there.

Shukhov had an idea. "I tell you what, Vanya, we'd better not carry it flat. Let's stand it on end, put an arm each around it, and just walk steadily with it hidden between us. If he's not too close, he'll be none the wiser."

It was a good idea. Getting an arm around the roll was awkward, though, so they just kept it pinned between them, like a third man, and moved off. From the side, all you could see was two men walking shoulder to shoulder.

"The site manager will catch on anyway as soon as he sees tar paper in the windows," Shukhov said.

Kildigs looked surprised. "So what's it got to do with us? When we turned up at the Power Station, there it was. Nobody could expect us to tear it down."

True enough.

Shukhov's fingers were frozen in those thin mittens, but his left boot was holding out. Boots were what mattered. Hands unstiffen once you start work.

They passed over a field of untrampled snow and came out onto a sled track leading from the tool shed to the Power Station. The cement must have been hauled along it.

The Power Station stood on a little hill, at the far end of the compound. Nobody had been near it for some time, and all the approaches were blanketed by a smooth layer of snow. The sled tracks, and a fresh trail of deep footprints, made by Gang 104, stood out all the more clearly. They were already at work with their wooden shovels, clearing a space around the plant and a path for the truck.

It would have been all right if the hoist had been working. But the engine had overheated and had never been fixed since. So they'd have to lug everything up to the second story themselves. Not for the first time. Mortar. Cinder blocks. The lot.

For two months the Power Station had stood abandoned, a gray skeleton out in the snow. But now Gang 104 had arrived. What kept body and soul together in these men was a mystery. Canvas belts were drawn tight around empty bellies. The frost was crackling merrily. Not a warm spot, not a spark of fire anywhere. All the same—Gang 104 had arrived, and life was beginning all over again.

The mortar trough lay in ruins right by the entrance to the generating room. It was a ramshackle thing. Shukhov had never had much hope that they'd get it there in one piece. The foreman swore a bit for the sake of appearances, but knew that nobody was to blame. Just then Kildigs and Shukhov rolled in, carrying the tar paper between them. The foreman brightened up and redeployed his men: Shukhov would fix the chimney pipe to the stove so that they could light a fire quickly, Kildigs would mend the mortar trough, with the two Estonians to help him, Senka Klevshin would get busy with his ax: the tar paper was only half the width of a window, and they needed laths to mount it on. But where would they come from? The site manager wouldn't issue boards to make a warm-up room. The foreman looked around, they all looked around. There was only one thing for it. Knock off some of the boards attached for safety to the ramps up to the second story. Nobody need fall off if he stepped warily. What else could they do?

Why, you may wonder, will a zek put up with ten years of backbreaking work in a camp? Why not say no and dawdle through the day? The night's his own.

It can't be done, though. The work gang was invented to take care of that. It isn't like a work gang outside, where Ivan Ivanovich and Pyotr Petrovich each gets a wage of his own. In the camps things are arranged so that the zek is kept up to the mark not by his bosses but by the others in his gang. Either everybody gets a bonus or else they all die together. Am I supposed to starve because a louse like you won't work? Come on, you rotten bastard, put your back into it!

When a gang feels the pinch as 104 did now, there's never any slacking. They jump to it, willy-nilly. If they didn't warm the place up in the next two hours, they'd all be done for, every last man.

Pavlo had brought the tools and Shukhov could help himself. There were a few lengths of piping as well, no tinsmith's tools, though. But there was a metalworker's hammer and a hatchet. He'd manage somehow.

Shukhov clapped his mittened hands together, then began fitting pipes by hammering the ends into shape. More hand-clapping. More hammering. (His trowel was hidden not far away. The other men in the gang were his friends, but they could easily take it and leave him another. Kildigs was no different from the rest.)

Every other thought went clean out of his head. He had no memory, no concern for anything except how he was going to join the lengths of pipe and fix them so that the stove would not smoke. He sent Gopchik to look for wire, so that he could support the chimney where it stuck out through the window.

There was another stove, a squat one with a brick flue, over in the corner. Its iron top got red-hot, and sand would thaw out and dry on it. This stove had already been lit, and the captain and Fetyukov were bringing in sand in a handbarrow. You don't need brains to carry a handbarrow. That's why the foreman had put these ex-bosses on the job. Fetyukov was supposed to have been a big boss in some office. Went around in a car.

When they first worked together, Fetyukov had tried throwing his weight around and shouting at the captain. But the captain smacked him in the teeth, and they called it quits.

Some of the men were sidling up to the stove with the sand on it, hoping for warmth, but the foreman warned them off.

"I'll warm one or two of you with my fist in a minute! Get the place fixed up first!"

One look at the whip is enough for a beaten dog! The cold was fierce, but the foreman was fiercer. The men went back to their jobs.

Shukhov heard the foreman speak quietly to Pavlo: "You hang on here and keep a tight hold on things. I've got to go and see about the percentages."

More depends on the percentages than the work itself. A foreman with any brains concentrates more on the percentages than on the work. It's the percentage that feeds us. Make it look as if the work's done, whether it is or not. If the rate for the job is low, wangle things so that it turns out higher. That's what a foreman needs a big brain for. And an understanding with the norm setters. The norm setters have their hands out, too.

Just think, though—who benefits from all this overfulfillment of norms? The camp does. The camp rakes in thousands extra from a building job and awards prizes to its lieutenants. To Volkovoy, say, for that whip of his. All you'll get is an extra two hundred grams of bread in the evening. But your life can depend on those two hundred grams. Two-hundred-gram portions built the Belomor Canal.[13]

Two buckets of water had been brought in, but they'd iced over on the way. Pavlo decided that there was no point in fetching any more. Quicker to melt snow on the spot. They stood the buckets on the stove.

Gopchik, who had pinched some new aluminum wire, the sort electricians use, had something to say: "Hey, Ivan Denisovich! Here's some good wire for spoons. Will you show me how to mold one?"

Ivan Denisovich was fond of Gopchik, the rascal (his own son had died when he was little, and he only had two grownup daughters at home). Gopchik had been jailed for taking milk to Ukrainian guerrillas hiding in the forest. They'd given him a grownup's sentence. He fussed around the prisoners like a sloppy little calf. But he was crafty enough: kept his parcels to himself. You sometimes heard him munching in the middle of the night.

Well, there wouldn't have been enough to go around.

---

13. **Belomor Canal** Canal system linking Baltic and White Seas, built, at great human cost, by convict labor in 1931–33.

They broke off enough wire for spoons and hid it in a corner. Shukhov rigged up a sort of ladder from two planks and sent Gopchik up to attach the chimney pipe. Gopchik was as light as a squirrel. He scrambled over the crossbeams, knocked in a nail, slung the wire over it, and looped it around the pipe. Shukhov had not been idle: he had finished the chimney with an elbow pipe pointing upwards. There was no wind, but there would be tomorrow, and he didn't want the smoke to blow down. They were fixing this stove for themselves, remember.

By then Senka Klevshin had split off some long strips of wood. They made Gopchik nail on the tarred paper. He scrambled up, the little imp calling down to them as he went.

The sun had hoisted itself higher and driven the mist away. The "posts" to either side of it were no longer visible, just the deep red glow between. They had gotten the stove going with stolen firewood. Made things a lot more cheerful.

"In January the sun warmed the cow's flanks," Shukhov commented.

Kildigs had finished knocking the mortar trough together. He gave a final tap with his ax and called out: "Hey, Pavlo, I want a hundred rubles from the foreman for this job, I won't take a kopeck less."

"You might get a hundred grams," Pavlo said, laughing.

"With a bonus from the prosecutor," Gopchik shouted from aloft.

"Don't touch it! Leave it alone," yelled Shukhov suddenly. They were cutting the tarred paper the wrong way.

He showed them how to do it.

Men had flocked around the sheet-metal stove, but Pavlo chased them away. He gave Kildigs some helpers and told him to make hods—they'd need them to get the mortar aloft. He put a few extra men on to carry sand. Others were sent up above to clear snow from the scaffolding and the brickwork itself. Another man, inside the building, was told to take the hot sand from the stove and tip it into the mortar trough.

An engine roared outside. They'd started bringing cinder blocks, and the truck was trying to get up close. Pavlo dashed out, waving his arms to show them where to dump the load.

By now they'd nailed on one width of tarpaper, then a second. What sort of protection would it give, though? Tarred or not, it was still just paper. Still, it looked like some sort of solid screen. And made it darker inside so the stove looked like it burned brighter.

Alyoshka had brought coal. "Throw it on!" some of them yelled, but others said, "Don't! We'll be warmer with just wood!" He stood still, wondering whom to obey.

Fetyukov had settled down by the stove and was shoving his felt boots— the idiot!—almost into the fire. The captain yanked him up by the scruff of the neck and gave him a push in the direction of the handbarrow.

"Go and fetch sand, you feeble bastard!"

The captain saw no difference between work in a camp and work on shipboard. Orders were orders! He'd gotten very haggard in the last month, the captain had, but he was still a willing horse.

Before too long, they had all three windows curtained with tar paper. The only light now came through the doors. And the cold came in with it. Pavlo ordered them to board up the upper part of the door space and leave the bottom so that a man could get in, stooping. The job was done.

Meanwhile, three truckloads of cinder blocks had been delivered and dumped. The question now was how to get them up to the second story without a hoist.

"Come on, men, let's get on with it!" Pavlo called to the bricklayers.

It was a job to take pride in. Shukhov and Kildigs went up after Pavlo. The ramp was narrow enough to begin with, and now that Senka had broken off the handrail, you had to hug the wall if you didn't want to land on your head. Worse still, snow had frozen onto the slats and made them round, so that there was no good foothold. How were they going to get the mortar up?

They took a look at the half-finished walls. Men were already shoveling snow from them, but would have to chip the ice from the old courses with hatchets and sweep it clear.

They worked out where they wanted the cinder blocks handed up, then took a look down. That was it—they'd station four men below to heave them onto the lower scaffolding, another two there to pass them up, and another two on the second floor to feed the bricklayers. That would still be quicker than lugging the things up the ramp.

On top the wind wasn't strong, but it never let up. It'll blow right through us, Shukhov thought, when we start laying. Still, if we shelter behind the part that's done already it'll be warmer, not too bad at all.

He looked up at the sky and gasped: it had cleared and the sun was nearly high enough for dinnertime. Amazing how time flew when you were working. He'd often noticed that days in the camp rolled by before you knew it. Yet your sentence stood still, the time you had to serve never got any less.

They went back down and found the rest all sitting around the stove, except for the captain and Fetyukov, who were still carrying sand. Pavlo lost his temper, chased eight men off to move cinder blocks, ordered two to pour cement into the mortar trough and dry-mix it with sand, sent one for water and another for coal. Kildigs turned to his detachment: "Right, boys, we've got to finish this handbarrow."

Shukhov was looking for work. "Should I give them a hand?" he asked.

Pavlo nodded. "Do that."

A tub was brought in to melt snow for mortar. They heard somebody saying it was twelve o'clock already.

"It's sure to be twelve," Shukhov announced. "The sun's over the top already."

"If it is," the captain retorted, "it's one o'clock, not twelve."

"How do you make that out?" Shukhov asked in surprise. "The old folk say the sun is highest at dinnertime."

"Maybe it was in their day!" the captain snapped back. "Since then it's been decreed that the sun is highest at one o'clock."

"Who decreed that?"

"The Soviet government."

The captain took off with the handbarrow, but Shukhov wasn't going to argue anyway. As if the sun would obey their decrees!

A few more bangs, a few more taps, and they had knocked four hods together.

"Right, let's sit down and have a warm," Pavlo said to the two bricklayers. "You as well, Senka—you'll be laying after dinner. Sit!"

So they got to sit by the stove—this time lawfully. They couldn't start laying before dinner anyway, and if they mixed the mortar too soon it would only freeze.

The coal had begun to glow and was giving off a steady heat. But you could only feel it by the stove. The rest of the room was as cold as ever.

All four of them took off their mittens and wagged their hands at the stove.

But—a word to the wise—don't ever put your feet near a fire when you're wearing boots or shoes. If they're leather shoes they'll crack, and if they're felt boots they'll steam and get damp and you won't be the least bit warmer. And if you hold them any nearer you'll burn them. And you won't get another pair, so you'll be tramping around in leaky boots till next spring.

"Shukhov's all right, though," Kildigs said, teasing him. "Know what, boys? He's got one foot out of here already."

Somebody took up the joke.

"Right, that foot, the bare one." They all burst out laughing. (Shukhov had taken the burnt left boot off to warm his foot rag.)

"Shukhov's nearly done his time," Kildigs said.

Kildigs himself was serving twenty-five years. In happier days everybody got a flat ten. But in '49 a new phase set in: everybody got twenty-five, regardless. Ten you could just about do without turning up your toes. But twenty-five?

Shukhov enjoyed it. He liked people pointing at him—see that man? He's nearly done his time—but he didn't let himself get excited about it. Those who'd come to the end of their time during the war had all been kept in, "pending further orders"—till '46. So those originally sentenced to three years did five altogether. They could twist the law any way they liked.

When your ten years were up, they could say good, have another ten. Or pack you off to some godforsaken place of exile.

Sometimes, though, you got thinking and your spirits soared: your sentence was running out, there wasn't much thread left on the spool! Lord! Just to think of it! Walking free, on your own two legs!

But it wouldn't be nice to say such things out loud to one of the old inhabitants. So Shukhov said to Kildigs: "Don't keep counting. Who knows whether you'll be here twenty-five years or not? Guessing is like pitch-forking water. All I know for sure is I've done a good eight."

When you're flat on your face there's no time to wonder how you got in and when you'll get out.

According to his dossier, Shukhov was in for treason. He'd admitted it under investigation—yes, he had surrendered in order to betray his country, and returned from POW camp to carry out a mission for German intelligence. What the mission could be, neither Shukhov himself nor his interrogator could imagine. They left it at that—just "a mission."

The counterespionage boys had beaten the hell out of him. The choice was simple enough: don't sign and dig your own grave, or sign and live a bit longer.

He signed.

What had really happened was this. In February 1942 the whole northwestern army was surrounded. No grub was being dropped by planes, and there were no planes, anyway. It got so bad that they were filing the hooves of dead horses, sousing the horny shavings in water, and eating them. They had no ammunition either. So the Germans rounded them up a few at a time in the forest. Shukhov was a prisoner in one such group for a couple of days, then he and four others escaped. They crawled about in the woods and marshes till they found themselves by some miracle among friends. True, a friendly tommy-gunner stretched two of them, and a third died from his wounds, so only two of them made it. If they'd had any sense they'd have said they'd got lost in the forest, and nothing would have happened to them. But they came out in the open: yes, we were taken prisoner, we've escaped from the Germans. Escaped prisoners, eh? . . . Nazi spies, more like! Behind bars is where you belong. Maybe if there'd still been five of them their statements would have been compared and believed. Just the two of them hadn't a chance: these two bastards have obviously worked out this escape story of theirs together.

Senka Klevshin made out through his deafness some talk about escaping and said loudly: "I've escaped three times and been caught three times."

The long-suffering Senka was mostly silent. Couldn't hear and didn't butt in. So nobody knew much about him except that he'd gone through Buchenwald, been in an underground organization there, and carried weapons into the compound for an uprising. And that the Germans had tied his hands behind his back, strung him up by his wrists, and thrashed him with canes.

Kildigs felt like arguing.

"So you've done eight, Vanya," he said, "but what sort of camps were you in? Ordinary camps, sleeping with women. You didn't wear numbers. You just try eight years' hard labor. Nobody's gone the distance yet."

"Women! Sleeping with logs, I was!"

Shukhov stared into the flames and his seven years in the north came back to him. Three years hauling logs for crates and rail ties to the log slide. The campfire at the tree-felling site was just like this one—now you saw it, now you didn't—and that was on night shift, not in the daytime. The big boss had laid down a law: any gang that didn't fulfill its daily quota stayed on after dark.

It would be past midnight when they dragged themselves back to camp, and they'd be off to the forest again next morning.

"No, friends," he lisped, "if you ask me, it's more peaceful here. We knock off on time—that's the law. Perhaps you've done your stint, perhaps you haven't, but it's back to the camp at quitting time. And the guaranteed ration is a hundred grams more. Life isn't so bad here. All right—it's a special camp. But why does wearing numbers bother you? They weigh nothing, number patches."

"More peaceful!" Fetyukov hissed. (It was getting near the dinner break, and they'd all found their way to the stove.) "People are getting their throats cut in bed. And he says it's more peaceful!"

Pavlo raised a threatening finger at Fetyukov. "Stoolies, not people!"

It was true. Something new had started happening in the camp. Two known stool pigeons had had their throats slit at reveille. Then the same thing had happened to an innocent working prisoner—whoever did it must have gotten the wrong bed. One stoolie had run off to the stone jailhouse for safety, and the bosses had hidden him there. Strange goings-on. There'd never been anything like it in ordinary criminal camps. But then it never used to happen in this one.

The power train's whistle suddenly blared. Not at the top of its voice to begin with, but with a hoarse rasping noise as though clearing its throat.

Midday! Down tools! Dinner-break!

"Damn, we've missed our chance! Should have gone to the mess and lined up a while ago."

There were eleven gangs at the site, and the mess would only hold two at a time.

The foreman still wasn't back: Pavlo took a quick look around and made up his mind.

"Shukhov and Gopchik—come with me. Kildigs—when I send Gopchik back, bring the team over right away."

Their places at the stove were grabbed immediately. Men hovered around the stove as though it was a woman they wanted to get their hands on.

There were shouts of "Wake up, somebody! Time to light up!"

They looked at each other to see who would get their cigarettes out. Nobody was going to. Either they had no tobacco or they were keeping it to themselves.

Shukhov went outside with Pavlo. Gopchik hopped along behind like a little rabbit.

"It's warmed up a bit," Shukhov decided. "Eighteen below, no more. Good weather for bricklaying."

They turned to look at the cinder blocks. The men had already dumped a lot of them on the scaffolding and hoisted some up to the planking on the second floor.

Shukhov squinted into the sun, checking out what the captain had said about the decree.

Out in the open, where the wind had plenty of room, it still nagged and nipped. Just in case they forgot it was January.

The work-site kitchen was a little matchwood hovel tacked together around a stove and faced with rusty tinplate to hide the cracks. Inside, a partition divided it into kitchen and eating area. The floors in kitchen and mess room alike were bare earth, churned up by feet and frozen into holes and hillocks. The kitchen was just a square stove with a caldron cemented onto it.

Two men operated the kitchen—a cook and a "hygienist."[14] The cook was given a supply of meal in the big kitchen before leaving camp in the morning. Maybe fifty grams a head, a kilo for every gang, say a bit less than a pood for the whole site. The cook wasn't going to carry a sack of meal that heavy for three kilometers, so he let his stooge do it. Better to give the stooge a bit extra out of the workers' rations than to break your own back. There were other jobs the cook wouldn't do for himself, like fetching water and firewood, and lighting the stove. These, too, were done by other people, workers or goners, and the cook gave each of them an extra portion, he didn't grudge what wasn't his own. Then again, men weren't supposed to take food out of the mess. Bowls had to be brought from camp (you couldn't leave them on the site overnight or the free workers would pinch them), and they brought only fifty, which had to be washed and passed on quickly. So the man who carried the bowls also had to be given an extra portion. Yet another stooge was posted at the door to see that bowls weren't carried out. But, however watchful he was, people would distract his attention or talk their way past him. So somebody had to be

---

14. **hygienist** A prisoner with no special training, appointed as a representative of the camp hospital.

sent around the site collecting dirty bowls and bringing them back to the kitchen. The man at the door got an extra portion. And so did the collector.

All the cook had to do was sprinkle meal and salt into the caldron and divide the fat into two parts, one for the pot and one for himself. (Good fat never found its way to the workers, the bad stuff went straight into the pot. So the zeks were happier when the stores issued bad fat.) Next, he stirred the gruel as it thickened. The "hygienist" did even less—just sat and watched. When the gruel was cooked, he was the first to be served: eat all your belly can hold. The cook did likewise. Then the foreman on duty would come along—the foremen did it in turn, a day at a time—to sample the stuff as if to make sure that it was fit for the workers to eat. He got a double portion for his efforts. And would eat again with his gang.

The whistle sounded. The work gangs arrived one after the other, and the cook passed bowls through his hatch. The bottom of each bowl was covered with watery gruel. No good asking or trying to weigh how much of your meal ration you were getting: there would be hell to pay if you opened your mouth.

The wind whistles over the bare steppe—hot and dry in summer, freezing in winter. Nothing has ever been known to grow on that steppe, least of all between four barbed-wire fences. Wheat sprouts only in the bread-cutting room, oats put out ears only in the food store. Break your back working, grovel on the ground, you'll never cudgel a scrap of food out of it. What the boss man doles out is all you will get. Only you won't get even that, what with cooks and their stooges and trusties. There's thieving on the site, there's thieving in the camp, and there was thieving before the food ever left the store. And not one of these thieves wields a pickax himself. You do that, and take what you're given. And move away from the serving hatch.

It's dog eat dog here.

When Pavlo entered the mess with Shukhov and Gopchik, men were standing on one another's feet—you couldn't see the sawn-off tables and benches for them. Some ate sitting down, but most of them standing. Gang 82, which had been sinking holes for fence posts all morning without a warm, had grabbed the first places as soon as the whistle went. Now even those who'd finished eating wouldn't move. They had nowhere to go. The others cursed them, but it was water off a duck's back—anything is more fun than being out in the freezing cold.

Pavlo and Shukhov elbowed their way through. They'd come at good time. One gang was just being served, there was only one other in line. Their deputy foremen were standing at the hatch. So all the other gangs would be behind 104.

"Bowls! Bowls!" the cook shouted from his hatch.

Bowls were passed through. Shukhov collected a few himself and shoved them at him—not in the hope of getting more gruel, but just to speed things up.

The stooges were washing bowls behind the screen—in return for more gruel.

The deputy foreman in front of Pavlo was about to be served. Pavlo shouted over the heads around him.

"Gopchik!"

"Here!" The thin little voice like the bleat of a goat came from near the door.

"Call the gang."

Gopchik ran off.

The great news was that the gruel was good today, the very best, oatmeal gruel. You don't often get that. It's usually *magara* or grits twice a day. The mushy stuff around the grains of oatmeal is filling, it's precious.

Shukhov had fed any amount of oats to horses as a youngster and never thought that one day he'd be breaking his heart for a handful of the stuff.

"Bowls! Bowls!" came a shout from the serving hatch.

104's turn was coming. The deputy foreman up front took a double foreman's portion and stopped blocking the hatch.

This was also at the workers' expense—and yet again nobody quibbled. Every foreman got the same and could eat it himself or pass it on to his assistant. Tyurin gave his extra portion to Pavlo.

Shukhov had his work cut out. He squeezed in at the table, shooed two goners away, asked one worker nicely, and made room for twelve bowls placed close together, with a second tier of six, and another two right on top. Then he had to take the bowls from Pavlo, check the count, and make sure no outsider rustled one from the table. Or jostled him and upset one. Meanwhile, other men were scrambling onto or off the bench, or sitting there eating. You had to keep an eye on your territory to make sure they were eating from their own bowls, not dipping into yours.

"Two, four, six," the cook counted behind his hatch. He handed two bowls at a time into two outstretched hands. One at a time might confuse him.

"Two! Four! Six!" Pavlo echoed in a low voice on the other side of the hatch, quickly passing two bowls at a time to Shukhov, who placed them on the table. Shukhov said nothing out loud, but kept a closer count than either of them.

"Eight, ten."

Where was Kildigs with the gang?

"Twelve, fourteen . . ." the count went on.

They'd run out of bowls in the kitchen. Shukhov saw, over Pavlo's shoulder, the cook's two hands put two bowls on the counter and pause as if in thought. He must have turned his head to curse the dishwashers. At that moment someone shoved a stack of emptied bowls through the hatch at him, and he took his hands off the bowls on the counter while he passed the empties back.

Shukhov abandoned the stock of bowls already on the table, stepped nimbly over the bench, whisked the two bowls from the counter, and repeated, not very loudly, as though it was meant for Pavlo, not the cook: "Fourteen."

"Hold it! where are you going with those?" the cook bellowed.

"He's my man, take it easy."

"All right, but don't try to confuse the count."

"It's fourteen," said Pavlo with a shrug. He'd never swipe an odd bowl himself, as deputy foreman he had to uphold authority, but this time he was only repeating what Shukhov had said and could blame him.

"I said fourteen before!" the cook said furiously.

"So what?" Shukhov yelled. "You said fourteen but you didn't hand 'em over, you never let go of 'em. Come and count if you don't believe me. They're all here on the table."

He could shout at the cook because he'd noticed the two Estonians pushing their way through to him, and shoved the two bowls into their hands as they came. He also managed to get back to the table and to do a quick count—yes, they were all there, the neighbors hadn't got around to pinching any, though there was nothing to stop them.

The cook's ugly red mug appeared in close-up through the hatch. "Where are the bowls?" he asked sternly.

"Look for yourself," Shukhov shouted. He gave somebody a push. "Out of the way, big boy, don't block the view. Here's two"—he raised the two second-story bowls an inch—"and there's three rows of four, dead-right, count them."

"Your gang not here yet?" The cook was staring suspiciously through the small opening. The hatch had been made narrow so that people couldn't peep through from the dining room and see how much was left in the caldron.

Pavlo shook his head. "No, they're not here yet."

"So what the hell do you mean by it, hogging bowls before the gang gets here?" The cook was beside himself with rage.

"Here they come now!" Shukhov shouted.

They could all hear the captain barking in the doorway as though he was still on the bridge of his ship: "Must you clutter up the place like this? Eat up, get out, and give somebody else a chance."

The cook growled a bit more. Then his face disappeared and his hands appeared at the hatch again.

"Sixteen, eighteen . . ." and, as he poured the last portion, a double one, "twenty-three! That's the lot! Next gang!"

As the gang shoved their way through, Pavlo passed the bowls, some of them over the heads of men already seated, to a second table.

In summer they could sit five to a bench, but now they were all wearing such bulky clothes there was hardly room for four, and even they had a job to use their spoons.

Taking it for granted that one of the bowls he'd swiped would be his, Shukhov quickly set about the one he'd earned by the sweat of his brow. This meant drawing his right knee up to his belly, unsheathing his "Ust-Izhma 1944" spoon from the leg of his boot, removing his cap and tucking it under his left arm, and running his spoon around the rim of the bowl.

This minute should have been devoted solely to the business of eating—spooning the thin layer of gruel from the bottom of the bowl, cautiously raising it to his mouth, and rolling it around with his tongue. But he had to hurry, so that Pavlo would see him finish and offer him the second portion. And then there was Fetyukov, who had arrived with the Estonians and had spotted him swiping the two bowls, and was now eating on his feet across the table from Pavlo, ogling the gang's four unallotted portions. This was a hint that he, too, expected a half portion if not a full one.

But Pavlo went on calmly eating his own double portion, and there was no knowing from the look on his swarthy young face whether he was aware of Fetyukov and remembered the two extra portions.

Shukhov had finished his gruel. Because he'd primed his stomach for two portions at once, it felt less full than usual after oatmeal. He reached into his inside pocket, took his unfrozen piece of round crust out of the rag, and carefully mopped the last remains of the oatmeal smear from the bottom and sides of the bowl. When he had collected enough, he licked the gruel from the crust and mopped up as much again. In the end the bowl was as clean as if it had been washed, except for a faint film. He passed it over his shoulder to the collector and sat a minute longer with his hat off.

It was Shukhov who had swiped the extra bowls, but the deputy foreman could do what he liked with them.

Pavlo tantalized him a bit longer while he finished his gruel, licked his spoon clean (but not the bowl), put it away safely, and crossed himself. Then he gave two of the four bowls a bit of a push—he was hemmed in too tightly to pass them—surrendering them to Shukhov.

"One for you, Ivan Denisovich, and one for Tsezar."

Shukhov hadn't forgotten that he would have to take one bowl to the office for Tsezar, who never lowered himself by coming to the mess, either on the site or in camp. But when Pavlo touched the two bowls at once his heart stood still: was he giving them both to Tsezar? Now his pulse was normal again.

He crouched over his lawful booty and ate thoughtfully, taking no notice of the newly arrived gangs shoving past behind him. His one worry was that Fetyukov might get a second bowl. Fetyukov hadn't the nerve to swipe anything for himself but he was a champion scrounger.

. . . Buynovsky was sitting a little way along the table. He had finished his gruel some time ago, didn't know that 104 had extra portions, and hadn't looked to see how many the deputy foreman had left. He had grown sluggish as he warmed up, and hadn't the strength to rise and go out into the cold air or to the chilly "warming shed" that warmed nobody. Now he was behaving like those he had tried to drive away with his metallic voice five minutes ago—taking up space to which he was not entitled and getting in the way of the gangs just arriving. He was new to camp life and to general duties. Moments like this, though he didn't know it, were very important to him: they were turning the loud and domineering naval officer into a slow-moving and circumspect zek: only this economy of effort would enable him to endure the twenty-five years of imprisonment doled out to him.

. . . People were pushing him from behind and yelling at him to give up his seat.

Pavlo spoke to him. "Captain! You there, Captain?"

Buynovsky started as if waking from a doze and looked around.

Pavlo held out the bowl of gruel without asking whether he wanted it.

Buynovsky's eyebrows rose, and he stared at the gruel as though it was an unheard-of-miracle.

"Go on, take it," Pavlo said reassuringly, then picked up the last bowl and carried it off to the foreman.

A guilty smile parted the captain's chapped lips. He had sailed all around Europe and across the Great Northern Sea Route, but now he bowed his head happily over less than a ladleful of thin gruel with no fat in it at all, just oats and water.

Fetyukov gave Shukhov and the captain an evil look and went out.

Shukhov himself thought it only right that the captain should get the spare portion. He might learn to look after himself someday, but so far, he had no idea.

Shukhov also had some faint hope that Tsezar would hand over his gruel. Though he had no call to, because he hadn't had a parcel for two weeks.

After his second portion Shukhov mopped the bottom and sides of the bowl, sucking his crust each time, as before, then finished off the crust itself. After which he picked up Tsezar's stone-cold gruel and left the mess.

"For the office," he said, pushing aside the stooge on the door, who didn't want to let him out with a bowl.

The office was a log cabin near the guardhouse. Smoke was still pouring from its chimney, as it had all morning. An orderly who also acted as their messenger kept the fire going. He was paid by the hour. The office was allowed any amount of kindling and firewood.

Shukhov opened a creaking door into a little lobby, then another door padded with oakum, and entered with a rush of frosty air, pulling the door to before anybody could shout "Shut it, clod!"

The office seemed to him as hot as a bathhouse. From the top of the Power Station the sun had looked cold and unfriendly: here it sparkled cheerfully through windows from which the ice was melting. Clouds of smoke from Tsezar's pipe floated in the sunlight like incense in church. The whole stove was aglow—the blockheads had gotten it red-hot. The chimney pipe was red-hot, too.

Sit down for a minute in that heat and you'd be fast asleep.

The office had two rooms. The door to the second, the site manager's room, was slightly ajar, and he was thundering:

"We're overspent on wages and we're overspent on building materials. Prisoners chop up expensive boards, and I don't mean just pre-fab panels, for firewood to burn in their shelters, and you turn a blind eye. The other day some prisoners were unloading cement outside the stores in a high wind and carrying it as much as ten meters on handbarrows, so the whole area around the stores was ankle-deep in the stuff and the workers left the site in gray instead of black. It's waste, waste, waste all the time!"

The manager was evidently in conference. With the overseers, no doubt.

A stupefied orderly was sitting on a stool in a corner by the entrance. Beyond him, Shkuropatenko, prisoner B-219, a crooked beanpole of a man, was staring through the window with his walleye, still trying to make out whether anybody was pinching his pre-fabs. The old fool had seen the last of his tar paper anyway.

Two bookkeepers, also zeks, were toasting bread on the stove. They'd rigged up a sort of wire griddle to keep it from burning.

Tsezar was lolling at his desk, smoking his pipe. He had his back to Shukhov and didn't see him.

Opposite him sat Kh-123, a wiry old man doing twenty years' hard. He was eating gruel.

"You're wrong, old man," Tsezar was saying, goodnaturedly. "Objectively, you will have to admit the Eisenstein is a genius. Surely you can't deny that *Ivan the Terrible* is a work of genius? The dance of the masked oprichniki![15] The scene in the cathedral!"

Kh-123's spoon stopped short of his mouth.

"Bogus," he said angrily. "So much art in it that it ceases to be art. Pepper and poppy seed instead of good honest bread. And the political motive behind it is utterly loathsome—an attempt to justify a tyrannical individual. An insult to the memory of three generations of the Russian intelligentsia!" (He was eating his gruel without savoring it. It wouldn't do him any good.)

"But would it have got past the censor if he'd handled it differently?"

---

15. **oprichniki** Members of a special armed force established by Ivan the Terrible, notorious for their indiscriminate ruthlessness.

"Oh well, if that's what matters . . . Only don't call him a genius—call him a toady, a dog carrying out his master's orders. A genius doesn't adjust his treatment of a theme to a tyrant's taste."

"Ahem!" Shukhov cleared his throat. He felt awkward, interrupting this educated conversation, but he couldn't just go on standing there.

Tsezar turned around and held his hand out for the bowl, without even looking at Shukhov—the gruel might have traveled through the air un-aided—then went back to his argument.

"Yes, but art isn't what you do, it's how you do it."

Kh-123 reared up and chopped at the table with his hand.

"I don't give a damn how you do it if it doesn't awaken good feelings in me!"

Shukhov stood there just as long as he decently could after handing over the gruel, hoping Tsezar would treat him to a cigarette. But Tsezar had entirely forgotten that Shukhov was behind him.

So he turned on his heel and left quietly.

Never mind, it wasn't all that cold outside. A great day for bricklaying.

Walking down the path, he spotted a bit of steel broken off a hacksaw blade lying in the snow. He had no special use for it right then, but you never knew what you might need later. So he picked it up and slipped it into his trouser pocket. Have to hide it in the Power Station. Thrift beats riches.

The first thing he did when he got back to the Power Station was find his trowel and shove it under the rope around his waist. Then he ducked into the mortar-mixing room.

Coming in from the sun, he found it quite dark, and no warmer than outside. The air was, if anything, rawer.

Men huddled next to the round stove rigged up by Shukhov, and the other stove on which thawing sand was steaming. While those who couldn't get close sat on the edge of the mixing trough. The foreman sat right by the fire, eating the last of his gruel. Pavlo had warmed it up for him on the stove.

A lot of whispering was going on, and the men were looking more cheerful. Somebody quietly gave Ivan Denisovich the news: the foreman had gotten a good rate for the job and had come back all smiles.

What work he could point to so far, only he knew. Half the day was gone and they'd done nothing. They wouldn't be paid for rigging up a stove and making themselves a warm shelter: that was work they did for themselves, not for the site. Something would have to be entered on the work sheet. Maybe Tsezar would slip in a few extras to oblige the foreman. The foreman treated Tsezar with respect, and he must have some reason for it.

"A good rate for the job" meant good rations for five days. Well, four days more likely: the bosses would appropriate one day's rations and hand out the standard minimum for every gang in the camp, good or bad. Fair shares all around, they called it—fair to everybody, but they were saving at the expense of the zek's belly. True enough, a zek's stomach can put up with anything: if today's no good, we'll stuff ourselves tomorrow. That was the dream the whole camp went to bed with on minimum-ration days.

Just think, though—it was five days' work and four days' eats.

The gang made little noise. Those who had tobacco took a few sly drags. Stared at the fire, huddled together in the half dark. Like a big family. That's what a work gang is—a family. They could hear the foreman yarning to two or three others near the stove. He never wasted words. If he was telling the tale, he must be in a good mood.

Andrei Prokofyevich Tyurin, the foreman, was another who hadn't learned to eat with his cap on. Without it, his head was an old man's. It was close-cropped, like everyone else's and you could see in the firelight a sprinkling of white hairs among the gray.

". . . I was scared even of the battalion commander, and this was the CO. 'Private Tyurin, reporting for orders,' I say. He fixes me with a stare from under his shaggy eyebrows and says, 'Name and patronymic?' I tell him. 'Year of birth?' I tell him. Well, what was I in 1930, I was all of twenty-two, just a pup. 'And who are you here to serve, Tyurin?' 'I serve the toiling people.' He boils over and bangs the desk with both hands. 'The toiling people! and what do you call yourself, you wretch?' It was like I'd swallowed something scalding. 'Machine-gunner, first-class,' I say. 'Passed with distinction in military and political subjects.' 'First-class, you vermin. Your father's a kulak![16] See this document—it's just come in from Kamen. You made yourself scarce because your father's a kulak. They've been after you for two years.' I turned pale and said nothing. I hadn't been writing home for a year in case they picked up the trail. I didn't know whether the family were alive or dead and they knew no more about me. 'Where's your conscience,' he roared, and the four bars on his shoulders were shaking, 'trying to deceive the workers' and peasants' government?' I thought he was going to beat me up. He didn't, though. He signed an order—gave me six hours to get out. It was November. They stripped me of my winter uniform and gave me a summer outfit, secondhand, socks that had done three tours of duty, a short-arsed greatcoat. I was a young fool; I didn't know I could have refused to turn the stuff in and sent them to hell. And I'd gotten this deadly entry in my papers: 'Discharged—son of a kulak.' Try and get a job with that in your record! I was four days from home by train, but they wouldn't issue me a travel pass, or a single day's rations. They just gave me one last dinner and booted me out of the depot.

---

16. **kulak** In the 1930s, this term was applied to all reasonably well-to-do peasants who were destined, by Stalin's order, to be "liquidated as a class."

"Incidentally, I met my old platoon commander in the Kotlas transit prison in '38, they'd slapped a tenner on him as well, and he told me the CO and the political commissar had both been shot in '37. Proletarians or kulaks, it made no difference in '37. Or whether or not they had a conscience . . . I crossed myself and said, 'So you're up there in heaven after all, Lord. You are slow to anger, but you hit hard.' "

After his two bowls of gruel, Shukhov was dying for a smoke. Telling himself that he would repay it when he bought the two tumblers of home-grown from the Latvian in Hut 7, he spoke quietly to the Estonian fisherman: "Listen, Eino, lend me enough for a cigarette till tomorrow. You know I won't let you down."

Eino looked Shukhov straight in the eye, then unhurriedly shifted his gaze to his so-called brother. They went halves in everything, and neither of them would lay out a shred of tobacco without asking the other. They muttered together, then Eino got out a pouch embroidered with pink thread. He took from it a pinch of factory-cut tobacco, put it on Shukhov's palm, sized it up, and added a few wisps. Just enough for rolling one cigarette, not a scrap more.

Shukhov had newspaper of his own. He tore a bit off, rolled his cigarette, picked up a hot ember that had landed between the foreman's feet, took a long drag, another long drag, and felt a sort of dizziness all over his body, as though drink had gone to his head and his legs.

The moment he lit up, green eyes glinted from the other side of the mixing room. Shukhov might have taken pity on Fetyukov and given him a drag, but he'd seen the scrounger score once that morning. Better to leave the butt for Senka Klevshin. The poor devil couldn't hear what the foreman was saying, he just sat with his head on one side, looking into the fire.

Firelight fell on Tyurin's pockmarked face. He told his story without self-pity. He could have been talking about somebody else.

"I sold what odds and ends I had to a secondhand dealer for a quarter of what it was worth, I bought a couple of loaves from under the counter—bread was rationed by then. I thought I could make my way home by jumping freight trains, but they'd strict laws against that as well—you could get shot trying it. And you couldn't get tickets, remember, even if you had money, and I hadn't. The streets around the station were chockablock with peasants in sheepskins. Some never got away, they died of hunger on the spot. All the tickets went to you-know-who—the OGPU, the army, people traveling on official business. You couldn't get on the platform either: there were militiamen at the doors, and security police footing it up and down the tracks on either side of the station. The sun was going down, it was cold, the puddles were icing over. Where could I spend the night? I somehow got a grip on the smooth stone wall, swung myself over with my loaves, and went into the station lavatory. I stood there a bit—nobody was after me. I walked out, trying to look like a passenger, just another soldier. And there on the tracks stood the Vladivostok–Moscow train. There was a crush around the hot-water boiler, people were passing their kettles over each other's heads. A girl in a dark blue blouse was hovering around with a two-liter kettle, afraid to get too close to the boiler. She had short little legs, and she was afraid she'd get scalded or trodden on. 'Here,' I said, 'hold my loaves and I'll get your hot water.' While I was filling up, the train started moving. She was holding my loaves, crying, she didn't know what to do with them. She didn't care about the kettle. 'Run,' I said, 'run for it, I'm right behind you!' She went ahead and I followed. I caught up with her, lifted her on the train with one hand—it was tearing along by then. I hoisted myself onto the step. The conductor didn't rap my fingers or punch me in the chest. There were other soldiers in the carriage and he mistook me for one of them."

Shukhov gave Senka a nudge, meaning finish this, poor devil. He even handed it over complete with his wooden holder—let him have a suck, it can't hurt me. Senka was a comic: he put one hand to his heart and bowed like an actor. He might be deaf, but he did his best.

The foreman went on with his story.

"There were some girls, six of them, traveling in a closed compartment. Leningrad students coming back from practical work. They'd got butter and I don't know what on the table, coats dancing away on hangers, suitcases in cloth covers. They didn't know they were living—they'd had green lights all the way. We got talking and joking and drinking tea together. Which carriage are you in? they asked. I sighed and came clean. 'It's a carriage to you, it could be a hearse to me,' I told them."

It was silent in the mixing room—just the stove crackling.

"They oohed and ahed, they had to talk it over . . . But they ended up hiding me under some coats on the top bunk. The conductors had OGPU men riding with them in those days. It wasn't just your ticket they wanted—it could be your skin. The girls kept me hidden and got me as far as Novosibirsk . . . Would you believe it, I had a chance later on to thank one of those girls. On Pechora. She'd caught it in the Kirov wave in '35,[17] she was on general duty, going down the drain fast, and I got her fixed up in the tailor's shop."

"Think we ought to make some mortar?" Pavlo asked in a whisper.

The foreman didn't hear him.

"I got to our house through the back gardens after dark. They'd whipped my father off already, and my mother and the little ones were waiting to be

---

17. The assassination of the high Party official Sergei Kirov in 1934 served as a pretext for a huge wave of arrests.

deported. A telegram had got there before me, and the village soviet was on the lookout. We were in a panic, we put the light out and sat on the floor against the wall—there were activists wandering around the village looking in at windows. That same night I grabbed my little brother and took him off somewhere warmer, to Frunze. There was nothing to eat, for him or me. I saw some young riffraff sitting around a tar boiler. I sat down by them and said, 'Listen, my bare-arsed friends, take my little brother as an apprentice, teach him how to live!' They took him . . . I now wish I'd joined the band of thieves myself."

"And you never saw your brother again?" the captain asked.

Tyurin yawned. "No, I never did." He yawned again and said, "Come on, boys, don't let it get you down! It's only a Power Station, but we'll make it a home away from home. Mortar mixers—get on with it. Don't wait for the whistle."

That's the beauty of a work gang. The big bosses can't make a zek hurry even in working hours, but if the foreman says work during the break, work it is. Because it's the foreman who feeds you. And besides, he won't make you do it unless it's necessary.

If the mixers waited for the whistle, the bricklayers would be at a standstill.

Shukhov sighed and stood up. "The ice has got to be cleared."

He took a hatchet and a brush for the ice, his gavel, his pole, his cord, and a plumb line.

Red-faced Kildigs gave Shukhov a sour look—why jump up before the foreman? It was all right for Kildigs—he didn't have to worry where the gang's next meal was coming from: two hundred grams of bread more or less didn't matter to the bald-headed so-and-so—he'd get by with his parcels.

He stood up all the same. He wasn't stupid. Knew he mustn't keep the whole gang waiting.

"Hold on, Vanya!" he called. "I'm with you."

You are now, chubby-cheeks. If you'd been working for yourself, you'd have been on your feet sooner.

(Shukhov had another reason for hurrying. They'd drawn only one plumb line from the tool store and he wanted to get hold of it before Kildigs.)

"Just the three of them laying?" Pavlo asked the foreman. "Or shall we put another man on? There might not be enough mortar, though."

The foreman frowned and thought for a bit.

"I'll be the fourth man, Pavlo! You see to the mortar. It's a big trough, so put six men on it, some can be taking mortar out of one half, and the rest mixing some fresh in the other. I don't want any holdups, not so much as a minute!"

"Right, then!" Pavlo sprang up. A young man, with fresh blood in his veins. The camps hadn't knocked the stuffing out of him yet. He'd gotten that fat face eating Ukrainian dumplings. "If you're going to lay yourself, I'll make mortar. Let's see who gets most done. Where's the longest shovel?"

That was the beauty of a work gang. You wouldn't expect a man like Pavlo, who'd sniped at people from the forest and raided Soviet towns at night, to break his back working in this place. But if it was for the foreman, that made all the difference.

Shukhov and Kildigs reached the top. They could hear Senka creaking up the ramp behind them, Deaf as he was, he'd gotten the message.

The second-floor walls hadn't got very far: they were three cinder blocks high all around, a bit higher in places. This was when the laying went best— from knee height up to your chest, without scaffolding.

There had been scaffold planks and trestles around earlier, but zeks had made off with the lot. Some they'd taken to other buildings, some they'd burned, anything as long as other gangs didn't get hold of them. If they planned it right, they'd have to knock some trestles together tomorrow or they'd be stuck.

You could see a long way from the top of the Power Station. The whole compound, covered with snow and deserted (the zeks were hiding in the warm till the whistle went). The dark towers. The sharp-pointed fence posts. The wire itself you could only see if you looked away from the sun, not into it. The sun was so bright it made you keep your eyes shut.

A little farther off, you could see the power-supply train. Look at all the smoke! Blackening the sky. The train started breathing hard. It always made that hoarse noise, like a man with a bad chest, before it whistled. There it was now. They hadn't got in much overtime.

Kildigs was hurrying him up.

"Hey you, Stakhanovite![18] Hurry up with that plumb line."

Shukhov jeered back at him.

"Look at all the ice on your wall! Think you'll get it chipped off before dark? Needn't have bothered bringing your trowel."

They were in position at the walls they'd settled on before dinner, but the foreman called out to them.

"Look, lads! We'll work in twos so the mortar won't freeze in the troughs. Shukhov, you have Klevshin on your wall and I'll work with Kildigs. And Gopchik can start by clearing Kildigs's wall for me."

Shukhov and Kildigs looked at each other. Good idea. Quicker that way. They grabbed their hatchets.

---

18. Stakhanovite A type of worker who voluntarily increased his productivity for the greater glory of communism. The term came into use in the 1930s.

And Shukhov no longer had eyes for the distant view, the glare of the sun on snow, the laborers struggling back from their warm hiding places to finish digging holes started that morning, or to strengthen the wire mesh for concrete, or put up trusses in the workshops. Shukhov saw only the wall in front of him, from the left-hand corner, where the brickwork rose in steps waist-high, to the right corner, where Kildigs's wall began. He showed Senka where to clear away the ice, and hacked away zealously himself, using blade and shaft by turns, so that ice splinters flew in all directions, sometimes hitting him in the face. He worked fast and skillfully, but without thinking about it. His mind and his eyes were studying the wall, the façade of the Power Station, two cinder blocks thick, as it showed from under the ice. Whoever had been laying there before was either a bungler or a slacker. Shukhov would get to know every inch of that wall as if he owned it. That dent there—it would take three courses to make the wall flush, with a thicker layer of mortar every time. That bulge couldn't be straightened out in less than two courses. He ran an invisible ruler over the wall, deciding how far he would lay from the stepped brickwork in the corner, and where Senka would start working toward Kildigs on his right. Kildigs wouldn't hold back at the corner, he decided, but would lay a few blocks for Senka to help him out. While they were tinkering in the corner, Shukhov would rush more than half the wall up, so he and Senka wouldn't be left behind. He sized up how many blocks he should have ready, and where. As soon as the laborers got up top with the blocks, he latched on to Alyoshka.

"Bring me mine! Put some here! And some over there!"

While Senka chipped away at the ice, Shukhov took his wire brush in both hands and scoured the wall all over, working specially hard on the grooves, leaving the upper course not quite clear, but with only a light film of frosted snow.

Shukhov was still scrabbling when the foreman climbed up and fixed his rod in the corner. Shukhov and Kildigs had put theirs up long ago.

Pavlo shouted from below: "Still alive up there? Mortar coming up!"

Shukhov broke out in a sweat: he hadn't put his string up yet. He decided to fix it for three courses at once, with a bit over. And to make it easier for Senka, he'd take in more of the outer course and leave him a bit more inside.

While he was tightening the string over the top edge, he explained to Senka with words and signs where he had to lay. The deaf man understood. Biting his lip and rolling his eyes, he nodded at the foreman's corner as much as to say, Let's give them hell! Let's beat them to it! He laughed.

The mortar was on its way up the ramp. Four pairs would be carrying it. The foreman decided not to set up troughs near the layers—the mortar would only freeze while it was being tipped into the troughs—but to put the handbarrows down by the men so they could help themselves. The carriers needn't hang around up top freezing, they could be shifting cinder blocks closer to the layers, instead. When the first two handbarrows were empty, a second lot would pass them on their way down, so there'd be no holdups. The first two pairs of carriers could make for the stove, defrost the lumps of mortar stuck to the handbarrows, and thaw themselves out if they had time.

The first two barrows arrived together, one for Kildigs's wall, one for Shukhov's. The mortar was barely warm, but it steamed in the frosty air. Slap it on and be quick about it or it'll freeze stiff and you'll have to break it up with your hammer, a trowel won't budge it. And if you lay a block the least bit out of line, it will freeze on, lopsided. All you can do then is knock it out with the head of your hatchet and chip the mortar away.

Shukhov didn't make mistakes, though. The blocks weren't all the same. If one of them had a corner knocked off or a kinky edge or a blister, Shukhov spotted it right away and knew which way around it needed to be laid and which spot in the wall was just waiting for it.

He scooped up a trowel full of steaming mortar, slapped it on the very spot, making a note where the blocks in the row below met so that the middle of the block above would be dead-center over the groove. He slapped on just enough mortar for one block at a time. Then he grabbed a block from the pile—he was a bit careful, though, he didn't want a hole in his mittens, and those blocks were horribly scratchy. Then he smoothed the mortar down with his trowel and plopped the block on it. Then, quick as quick, he squared it up, tapping it into place with the side of his trowel if it wasn't sitting right, making sure it was flush with the outside of the wall and dead-level widthwise and lengthwise. Because it would freeze on and stick fast right away.

Next, if any mortar had been squeezed out from under the block, you had to chip it off quick and flick it away with your trowel. (In summer you could use it for the next block, but this time of year—forget it.) Then another look at the bonding in the row below—there might be a damaged block, where a bit had crumbled away, and if there was, you slapped on more mortar, thicker under the left end, and didn't just lay the block but slid it on from right to left so it squeezed out the extra mortar between itself and the block to the left. Make sure it's flush. Make sure it's flat. Block set fast. Next, please!

Off to a good start. Get two courses laid and tidy up the old rough bits and it's all plain sailing. Keep your eyes skinned, now!

Shukhov was rushing the outer course to join up with Senka. And Senka, in the corner with the foreman, was letting it rip on his way toward Shukhov.

Shukhov signaled to the carriers—mortar, quick, over here where I can reach it! Haven't even got time to wipe my nose!

Shukhov and Senka met up, started dipping into the same barrow, and scraped bottom.

"Mortar!" Shukhov roared over the wall.

"Coming!" Pavlo yelled back.

Fresh mortar was brought. They scooped up all the moist stuff, but the carriers would have to scrape off what had stuck to the sides. If they let a thick crust grow, they were the ones who'd be lugging all that extra weight up and down. Right, you can push off! Next, please!

Shukhov and the other layers had stopped feeling the cold. Once they got into their stride, that first glow passed over them—the glow that makes you wet under jacket, jerkin, overshirt, and undershirt. But they didn't let up for a single moment, they went on laying faster and faster, and an hour later the second glow hit them, the one that dries the sweat. The frost wasn't getting at their feet, that was the main thing, nothing else, not even that thin, nagging wind could take their minds off their work. Klevshin, though, kept knocking one foot against the other. He took size 11, poor devil, and the boots they'd given him weren't a pair but were both too tight.

Every now and then the foreman yelled "Mortar," and Shukhov echoed him. Set a brisk pace and you become a sort of foreman yourself. Shukhov wasn't going to fall behind the other two: to hurry the mortar up that ramp, he'd have run the legs off his own brother.

After the dinner break Buynovsky had begun by working with Fetyukov. The ramp was steep and treacherous and he didn't make a very good job of it to begin with. Once or twice Shukhov gave him a gentle touch of the whip.

"Hurry it up a bit, Captain! Captain, let's have some blocks here!"

But while the captain moved more briskly with every load, Fetyukov got lazier: the shitbag would walk along, deliberately tilting the handbarrow and splashing mortar out to make it lighter.

Once Shukhov punched him in the back.

"Filthy rat! I bet you kept the men hard at it when you were the manager!"

"Foreman!" the captain shouted. "Put me with a human being! I refuse to work with this prick!"

The foreman made the switch. Fetyukov could heave blocks onto the scaffolding from below, where they could count separately how many he shifted, and Alyoshka the Baptist would work with the captain. Anybody who felt like it could order Alyoshka about, he was so meek and mild.

The captain kept egging him on. "Heave-ho, me hearties! Look how fast they're laying those blocks!"

Alyoshka smiled humbly. "We can go faster if you like. Whatever you say."

They trudged down the ramp.

A meek fellow like that is a treasure to his gang.

The foreman shouted down to somebody. Another truck carrying cinder blocks had just pulled up. Not a sign of one for six months, then they come in droves. Work all out while they're bringing them. There'll be holdups later and you'll never get back into the swing of it.

The foreman was at it again, cursing somebody down below. Something to do with the hoist. Shukhov was curious but too busy straightening out the wall. The mortar carriers came over and told him: a mechanic had arrived to repair the engine on the hoist, and the man in charge of electrical work, a free employee, was with him. The mechanic was tinkering and the free man was watching him.

Normal, that: one working, one watching.

If they hurry up and fix the hoist, we can lift the mortar and the cinder blocks with it.

Shukhov was well on with the third row (and Kildigs had just started his third) when yet another watchdog, another boss man, started up the ramp—Der, the overseer of building works. A Muscovite. Supposed to have worked in a ministry.

Shukhov, close to Kildigs by now, pointed at Der.

"So what?" Kildigs said. "I never have anything to do with the bosses. Call me, though, if he falls off the ramp."

Now he'd be standing behind the layers, watching. If there was one thing Shukhov couldn't endure, it was these spectators. Trying to wangle himself an engineer's job, the pig-faced bastard. Started showing me how to lay blocks once. Laughed myself sick. Till you've built one house with your own hands, you're no engineer. That's how I see it.

They didn't have brick buildings in Temgenyovo, the cottages were all built of wood. Even the school was a log cabin—they'd brought ten-meter tree trunks from the state forest. But when the camp suddenly needed a bricklayer—Shukhov thought he might as well be one. If you can do two things with your hands, you'll soon pick up another ten.

Pity, Der tripped once but didn't fall off. Reached the top almost at a run.

"Tyu-u-rin!" he yelled, with his eyes popping out. "Tyurin!"

Pavlo came running up the plank behind him, still gripping his shovel.

Der's jacket was camp-issue, but a nice, clean, newish one. He was wearing a splendid leather cap. But it had a number on it, like everybody else's. B-731.

"What do you want?" Tyurin went to meet him, trowel in hand. His cap had slipped down over one eye.

Must be something special. Shukhov didn't want to miss it, but the mortar was getting cold in the trough. He went on laying while he listened.

"What the hell do you mean by it?" Der was yelling, spittle flying. "You're asking for more than a spell in the hole! This is a criminal offense, Tyurin! You'll get a third term!"

Shukhov suddenly caught on. He shot a glance at Kildigs. Kildigs had realized it, too. The tar paper! Der had spotted the tarred paper over the window spaces.

Shukhov wasn't afraid for himself. The foreman wouldn't give him away. It was the foreman he was afraid for. Like a father to us, the foreman is. Just a pawn to them. For this sort of thing they'd just as soon fix him up with another stretch in the Arctic as not.

Shukhov had never seen the foreman look so ugly. He threw his trowel down with a clatter. Took a step toward Der. Der looked behind him—there was Pavlo, shovel in the air.

Of course! He'd brought it up on purpose.

And Senka, deaf as he was, had realized what was going on, and moved in with his hands on his hips. A tough old devil he was, too.

Der blinked and looked around nervously for a bolt-hole.

The foreman put his face close to Der's. He was speaking quietly, but his voice carried up top there.

"The time's gone when a shit like you could hand out sentences. Say a single word, you bloodsucker, and your last day's come. Just you remember!"

The foreman was trembling all over. Couldn't stop trembling.

And the look on Pavlo's sharp features would cut a man in two.

Der turned pale and moved away from the ramp.

"Steady on, boys! Take it easy!" he said.

The foreman said no more, but straightened his cap, picked up his curved trowel, and went back to his wall.

Pavlo walked slowly down the plank with his shovel.

Real slow.

Oh, yes. Slitting a few throats had made a difference. Just three of them—and you wouldn't know it was the same camp.

Der was afraid to stay, and afraid to go down. He stood still, hiding behind Kildigs's back.

Kildigs went on laying, like somebody weighing out medicine at the chemist's. He looked like a doctor, and he always took his time. He kept his back to Der, pretending he hadn't seen him.

Der crept over to the foreman. No bossiness about him now.

"What can I tell the site manager, Tyurin?"

The foreman went on laying and didn't look around.

"Tell him it was there already. Like that when we got here."

Der hung around a bit more. He could see they weren't about to kill him there and then. He strolled around quietly, with his hands in his pockets.

"Hey, Shcha-854," he growled. "Why are you putting the mortar on so thin?"

He had to take it out on somebody. And since nobody could find fault with Shukhov's bonding, he had to say the mortar was too thin.

"With your permission," Shukhov lisped, with a bit of a grin, "if I lay it any thicker, this Power Station will be letting in water all over next spring."

"You're just a bricklayer—you'd better listen to what your overseer tells you."

Der frowned and puffed out his cheeks—a habit of his.

Well, maybe it was a bit thin in places. Might have been thicker if we'd been working like human beings, not out here in the middle of winter. You ought to show a bit of consideration. We've got to earn all we can. No good trying to explain, though, if he can't see it himself.

Der went quietly down the ramp.

"You get my hoist fixed up!" the foreman shouted after him. "What do you take us for—cart horses? Heaving cinder blocks up two stories by hand!"

"You'll be paid for it!" Der answered, from halfway down—but peaceably.

"Wheelbarrow rate, I suppose? Go on, get hold of a wheelbarrow and try running it up that ramp. We want handbarrow rate!"

"I wouldn't grudge you. But Accounts won't put it through at handbarrow rate."

"To hell with Accounts! I've got my whole gang carrying for four bricklayers. How much can I earn that way?"

The foreman went on laying steadily while he was shouting.

"Mor-tar!" he shouted down.

Shukhov took up the cry. "Mor-tar!" Finished leveling up the third row, now get going on the fourth. Ought really to take the string a course higher, but it'll do. We can rush up one course without it.

Der was away across the site, all hunched up. Heading for the office to get warm. Feeling a bit uncomfortable, I bet. Ought to stop and think before he takes on a wolf like the foreman. Keep on good terms with Tyurin and his like and he wouldn't have a care in the world. Nobody expects him to break his back, he gets big rations, lives in a cabin of his own—what more does he want? Wants to show how clever he is, that's what.

Somebody came up the ramp to say that the manager (electrical maintenance) and the mechanic had both left, and the hoist couldn't be mended.

So—donkey work it is.

Every job Shukhov had been on, either the machinery broke down or else the zeks broke it. A conveyor, say, they'd wreck by ramming a rod through the chain and putting on the pressure. Just to get a rest. If you're made to stack peeled logs all day, bent double, you can get stuck that way.

"More blocks!" the foreman shouted. He was in top gear now. The heavers and carriers got called everything under the sun.

Loud voices from below. "Pavlo says what about mortar."

"Mix some, what do you think."

"We've still got half a trough left."

"So mix another."

It was going like a house on fire. They were on the fifth course. They'd had to do the first doubled up, but the wall was breast-high now, or nearly. Nothing to it, anyway—no windows, no doors, just two blank walls, joining up, and plenty of cinder blocks. Should have raised the string—too late now.

"Gang 82 are handing their tools in," Gopchik reported.

The foreman flashed a look at him. "Mind your own business, small-fry, and get some blocks over here."

Shukhov looked over his shoulder. Yes, the sun was going down. A reddish sun in a sort of grayish mist. We're really getting somewhere now. Couldn't be better. On the fifth course now, so we'll just finish it off. Then level it all up.

The carriers sounded like cart horses out of breath. The captain's gray in the face. Well, he must be forty, or getting on that way.

It was some degrees colder already. Shukhov's hands were busy, but the cold nipped his fingers through the thin mittens. And sneaked into his left boot. He stamped his foot now and then to warm it.

He could work on the wall without crouching now, but had to bend his aching back for every cinder block and every spoonful of mortar.

"Come on, boys," he said roughly. "You could put the blocks up here on the wall for me."

The captain would have obliged, only he hadn't the strength. Wasn't used to it. But Alyoshka said: "Right, then, Ivan Denisovich. Just show me where you want them."

Never says no, that Alyoshka, whatever you ask him to do. If everybody in the world was like him, I'd be the same. Help anybody who asked me. Why not? They've got the right idea, that lot.

The clanging of the hammer on the rail carried across the whole site as far as the Power Station. Knocking-off time. Just when the mortar was made. That's what comes of trying too hard.

"Mortar! Let's have some mortar!" the foreman yelled.

A new batch had just been made. Nothing for it now—just keep on laying. If we don't empty the trough, it'll be the devil's own job cracking it tomorrow. The mortar will be stone-hard, you won't gouge it out with a pickax.

"Don't give up yet, boys!" Shukhov urged.

Kildigs looked angry. He didn't like rush jobs. Back home in Latvia, he said, everybody took his time and everybody was well off. But there was no getting out of it. He had to step on it, like the rest of them.

Pavlo hurried up top between the shafts of a handbarrow, bringing his trowel. He joined the bricklayers. Five trowels at work now. Just time enough to center blocks over the joints below. Shukhov would quickly size up the block needed in each case and shove a gavel at Alyoshka.

"Here—square it up for me."

More haste, less speed. Now that the others were out to break records, Shukhov stopped forcing the pace and took a good look at the wall. He steered Senka to the left and took the right, over toward the main corner, himself. To leave a bulge in the wall or make a mess of the corner would be a disaster. Take half of tomorrow to put it right.

"Hold it!" He came between Pavlo and the block he was laying and straightened it himself. Looks as if Senka's got a dent near the corner there. He darted over and straightened two blocks.

The captain hauled another load in like a willing horse.

"There's another two barrowloads to come," he shouted.

On his last legs, but still pulling his weight. Shukhov's gelding, the one he had before collectivization, had been the same. Shukhov had taken good care of him, but when strangers got their hands on him, they worked him to a frazzle. And did him in in no time.

The rim of the sun had disappeared behind the earth now. Shukhov could see for himself, without Gopchik telling him, that all the other gangs had handed their tools in and men were flocking toward the guardhouse. (Nobody went outside the moment "down tools" was sounded. They weren't daft enough to stand out there freezing. They sat around in their warm corners for a bit. But at a certain moment the foreman would agree to move and the gangs streamed out all at once. They had to do it that way because convicts are such a pigheaded lot they'd be there till midnight seeing who could sit in the warm longest.)

Tyurin realized that he'd left it a bit late. The toolmaker would be calling him every name he could lay his tongue to.

"Right," he said. "No good saving shit! Hodmen—whizz down, scrape out the big trough, carry the lot to that hole over there, and shovel snow on top so nobody can see it. You, Pavlo, take two men, collect the tools, and hand them in. I'll send Gopchik after you with the three trowels once we've got through the last couple of barrowloads of mortar."

They jumped to it. Took Shukhov's gavel from him, untied his string. The hodmen and brick heavers all hurried down to the mixing room—nothing left for them to do up top. Only the three bricklayers—Kildigs, Klevshin, and Shukhov—stayed behind. The foreman walked around checking what they'd done. Seemed pleased.

"Good bit of bricklaying, eh? For half a day's work. Without a hoist, or any other effing thing."

Shukhov saw that Kildigs had only a bit left in his trough. But he was worried that the foreman would get in a row in the tool store for keeping the trowels back. He found the answer.

"Listen, men, go ahead and take your trowels to Gopchik, mine isn't counted, and I don't have to hand it in, so I can finish the job."

The foreman laughed. "They'd be crazy to let you out! Any jail would be lost without you!"

Shukhov laughed back at him. And went on laying.

Kildigs carried the trowels away. Senka fed cinder blocks to Shukhov. They tipped Kildigs's mortar into Shukhov's trough.

Gopchik ran all the way to the tool store, trying to catch up with Pavlo. And Gang 104 set out across the site by itself, without its foreman. A foreman carries a lot of weight—but the convoy guards carry more. They'll make note of latecomers—and pack them off to the hole.

The crowd by the guardhouse had thickened alarmingly. Everybody was there by now. Looked as if the guard had turned out, too, to count them all again.

(They count twice at every turnout. Once with the gates shut to find out whether it's safe to open them, the second time as the men are passing through the gates. And if they fancy they see anything wrong, they count yet again outside the gates.)

"To hell with the mortar," the foreman said impatiently. "Chuck it over the wall!"

"Better be off, foreman! You're needed there more!" (Shukhov generally called him Andrei Prokofyevich, but working as he was now made him the foreman's equal. He didn't put it in words to himself—"I'm as good as he is"—just felt it.) "Bloody nuisance, these short working days," he called out jokingly, as the foreman strode down the ramp. "Just when you're beginning to enjoy yourself, it's quitting time."

Only himself and the deaf man left. No good talking to him. No need, anyway: he's cleverer than the lot of them, you never have to tell him anything.

Slap on the mortar! Slap on a block! Press it down a bit. Make sure it's straight. Mortar. Block. Mortar. Block.

The foreman had ordered them not to worry about wasting mortar, to chuck it over the wall and take off. But Shukhov was the sort of fool who couldn't let anything or anybody's work go to waste, and nobody would ever teach him better.

Mortar! Block! Mortar! Block!

"Enough, damn it!" Senka shouted. "Time to be off!"

He grabbed a handbarrow and was away down the ramp.

If the guards had set their dogs on him, it wouldn't have stopped Shukhov. He moved quickly back from the wall to take a good look. All right. Then quickly up to the wall to look over the top from left to right. Outside straight as could be. Hands weren't past it yet. Eye as good as any spirit level.

He ran down the ramp.

Senka came running out of the mixing room and up the slope. Turned his head to shout.

"Come *on!*"

"Keep running. I won't be a minute."

Down into the mixing room. Can't just leave the trowel lying around. Might not be brought out tomorrow. They might pack the gang off to Sotsgorodok. Could be six months before I get back to this place. I'm not going to let that trowel get lost. Hide it, then, and hide it good and proper!

All the stoves were out in the mixing room. It was dark. He felt afraid. Not because of the dark, but because everybody had gone, he'd be the only one missing at the guardhouse, and the guards would pitch into him.

Still—take a good look around. He spotted a hefty stone up a corner, rolled it over, shoved the trowel behind, and covered it. Okay now!

Quick, catch up with Senka. He's only run a hundred yards. Wouldn't go any farther without me. Never leave anybody in the lurch, Senka wouldn't. If there's going to be trouble, we're in it together—that's Senka.

They ran side by side, the big man and the shorter man. Senka was head and shoulders taller than Shukhov, and it was a huge head he had on him.

Some people with nothing better to do run races in stadiums of their own free will. Silly devils should try running for their lives, bent double after a day's work. In this cold, with wet mittens and worn-out boots.

Shukhov and Senka were as hot as rabid dogs. Their own panting was all they could hear.

Still, the foreman was at the guardhouse, he'd explain.

They were running straight toward the crowd, and it was scary.

Hundreds of raucous voices started baying at them: cursing them up and down and calling them all the bastards in creation. Who wouldn't be scared with five hundred furious men yelling at him!

What mattered, though, was how the guards would take it.

The guards weren't bothered. The foreman was right there, in the back row. He must have explained, taken the blame on himself.

The men went on yelling and cursing horribly. Yelling so loud that even Senka heard quite a bit; he took a deep breath and roared back. He lived his life in silence—but when he did sound off . . . ! He put up his fists, spoiling for a fight. The men stopped shouting, and some of them laughed.

"Hey, 104! Thought you said he was deaf!" they called out. "We wanted to make sure."

Everybody laughed. Guards as well.

"Form up in fives!"

They weren't opening up, though. Didn't trust themselves. They pushed the crowd back. (The idiots were all glued to the gates as though that would speed things up.)

"By-y fives! First! Second! Third!"

As they called out each five, it moved forward a few meters.

While this was going on, Shukhov got his breath back and looked around. Old Man Moon was right up there now, red and sulky-looking. Just past the full. Yesterday it had been a lot higher at that time.

Shukhov felt playful now that everything had gone so smoothly. He nudged the captain and shot a question at him. "Here, Captain, you know science—where does it say the old moon goes?"

"What do you mean, where does it go? What an ignorant question! It's there, we just can't see it."

Shukhov wagged his head and laughed. "So, if you can't see it, how do you know it's there?"

The captain looked surprised. "According to you, then, the moon really is new every month?"

"What's so strange about that? People are born every day, why shouldn't a moon be born every four weeks?"

The captain spat in disgust. "I never met a sailor as stupid as you. Where do you think the old moon goes, then?"

"That's what I'm asking you—where does it go?" Shukhov showed his teeth.

"Go on, tell me."

Shukhov sighed and delivered his reply with a slight lisp. "Where I come from, they used to say God breaks up the old moon to make stars."

The captain laughed. "What savages! I never heard anything like it! So you believe in God, do you, Shukhov?"

Now Shukhov was surprised. "Of course I do. How can anybody not believe in God when it thunders?"

"Why does God do it, then?"

"Do what?"

"Break up the moon to make stars. Why, do you think?"

"That's an easy one," Shukhov said with a shrug. "Stars fall every now and then, the holes have to be filled up."

"Turn around, goddamn you!" the guards were shouting. "Get lined up!"

The count had reached them. The twelfth row of five after four hundred went through with two men behind them, Buynovsky and Shukhov.

The guards were flummoxed. Consulted their tally boards. A man short again! The rotten dogs might at least learn how to count!

They'd counted 462 and they told each other it should be 463.

The men had pressed forward to the gate again, and once again they were shoved back and it was:

"Form up in fives! First five! Second!"

The time wasted on these recounts of theirs was not the state's but the men's own—that's what made it all so vexatious. They still had to trudge over the steppe back to camp and line up outside for the body search. Men from all the different sites would be racing to be searched first and dive into camp before all the others. Whichever work party arrived first was king for the day: the mess hut would be waiting, they'd have first chance to claim parcels, be first at the storeroom, first at the individual kitchen, first at the CES[19] to collect letters or hand in their own to be censored, first at the sick bay, the barber's, the bathhouse—everywhere.

Generally, the guards were in just as much of a hurry to get the men off their hands and withdraw to their own quarters. A soldier couldn't afford to hang about, either: there was too much to do and too little time for it.

But the figures didn't add up.

As they were waving the last rows of five past, Shukhov thought for a moment that there would be three of them right at the back. But no—it was still only two.

The counters hurried over to the guard commander with their boards. There was some talk, then the commander yelled out: "Foreman Gang 104!"

Tyurin took half a step forward. "Here."

"Any of yours left behind at the Power Station? Think before you answer."

"No."

"Think, or I'll tear your head off!"

"It's like I said."

But he shot a glance at Pavlo—maybe somebody had gone to sleep back there in the mixing room?

"Form up by gangs!" the guard commander shouted.

The gangs had been mixed together. When they formed fives, each man had just moved up to whoever was nearest. Now there was a lot of shoving and shouting "76—this way!" "13—over here!" "Come on, 32!"

104 stayed where it was, behind all the rest. Shukhov was now able to see that the whole gang was empty-handed. The idiots had been working so hard they hadn't collected any kindling. Only two of them had dainty little bundles.

This was a game they played every day. Before quitting time, the workers would collect wood chips, sticks, bits of broken board, and carry them off tied up with a strip of rag or a bit of string. The first raid might come at the guardhouse. If the site manager or one of the overseers was waiting there, he would order them to drop the lot. (As if by collecting wood chips they could make up for the millions they'd sent up in smoke.) But the workers had

---

19. **CES** Cultural and Educational Section.

ideas of their own. If every man in a gang got home with just a stick or two, the hut would be that much warmer. Without this, there was only the five kilograms of coal dust issued to the hut orderlies for each stove, and you couldn't expect much warmth from that. So besides the wood they carried in their hands they broke or sawed sticks into short pieces and stuffed them under their jackets. That much they'd get past the site manager.

The guards never ordered them to drop their firewood on the work site. The guards also needed firewood, and couldn't carry it themselves. For one thing, their uniform forbade it, and for another, their hands were full with the automatic weapons they needed to shoot prisoners. But when they'd marched the column up to the camp, they'd give the order: "All those from row such-and-such to row such-and-such, drop your wood over here." They weren't heartless, though: they had to leave some wood for the warders, and some for the zeks themselves, otherwise nothing at all would be brought in.

So the rule was that every zek carried some firewood every day. Sometimes you'd get it home, sometimes it would be taken from you. You never knew.

While Shukhov's eyes were combing the ground looking for chips to pick up, the foreman counted the gang and reported to the guard commander: "104—all present!"

Including Tsezar, who had left the other office workers and joined his own gang. There was hoarfrost on his black mustache. He puffed hard at his pipe and the red glow warmed his face.

"How are things, Captain?" he asked.

Stupid question! If you're warm yourself, you don't know what it's like freezing.

The captain shrugged. "How do you think? I've worked so hard I can hardly stand up straight."

Meaning you might at least give me a smoke.

Tsezar offered him a smoke. The captain was the only one in the gang he hobnobbed with. There was nobody else he could have a heart-to-heart talk with.

"One missing in 32!" Everybody took up the cry.

The deputy foreman of Gang 32 and another fellow peeled off to search the motor-repair shops.

A buzz went through the crowd. What was it? What was he up to? The word reached Shukhov that it was the little dark Moldavian. Which Moldavian was that? The one they said was a Romanian spy? A real spy, for once.

There were five spies in every gang, but those were made-up spies, make-believe spies. Their papers had them down as spies, but they were just ex-prisoners of war. Shukhov was one of those himself.

That Moldavian, though, was the real thing.

The guard commander took one look at his list and went black in the face. He was in for it if a spy had escaped!

The whole crowd, Shukhov as well, were furious. What sort of rotten creep, louse, shit, swine, murdering bastard was he? The sky was dark, what light there was must be coming from the moon, the frost was hardening for the night, and that mangy cur was missing! Hadn't the shit had his fill of work? Wasn't the official working day, eleven hours of it from dawn to dusk, long enough for him? Just you wait! The Prosecutor will find you some extra time!

Even Shukhov thought it weird—working and not noticing the signal.

He'd quite forgotten that he'd just been doing it himself and had felt peeved when he saw them all crowding around the guardhouse too early. Now he was freezing with the rest, and fuming with the rest, and thinking that if that Moldavian kept them waiting another half hour, and the guards handed him over to the crowd, they'd tear him to pieces like wolves tearing a calf!

Now the cold was really biting! Nobody could keep still—they were all stamping their feet, or taking two steps forward, two steps back.

People were wondering whether the Modavian could be trying to escape. If he'd run off earlier in the day, that was one thing, but if he was hiding and waiting for the guards to be brought down from the watchtowers, he'd wait in vain. If there were no tracks showing where he'd crawled under the wire, they'd keep the guards up there for three whole days while they searched the whole site. Or a week, if need be. Any old convict knows that's what standing orders say. One way or another, the guards' life isn't worth living with somebody on the loose. They're run off their feet, can't stop to eat or sleep. Sometimes they get so furious that the runaway isn't brought back alive. They shoot him down.

Tsezar was working on the captain.

"The pince-nez dangling from the rigging, for instance—remember?"[20]

"Mm—yes." The captain was busy smoking.

"Or the baby carriage rolling and rolling down the Odessa steps?"

"Yes. But, in that film, life on board ship is like a puppet show."

"Maybe modern film technique makes us expect too much."

"The officers are rotters to a man."

"That's true to history!"

"So who do you think led the men into battle? Then again, those maggots crawling on the meat look as big as earthworms. Surely there were never any maggots like that?"

"The camera can't show them any smaller!"

---

20. Further comment on Eisenstein's *Potemkin*.

"I tell you what, if they brought that meat to our camp today instead of the shitty fish we get and chucked it in the pot without washing or scraping it, I think we'd . . ."

Cries came from the zeks. "Aaaah! Ooooh!"

They'd seen three figures darting out of the auto-repair shop. Evidently the Moldavian had been found.

The crowd by the gate howled. "Oo-oo-oo-ooh."

Then when the three got closer:

"Filthy swine! Traitor! Rat! Dirty dog! Shitface! Rotten bastard!"

Shukhov joined in:

"Filthy swine!"

Well, it was no joke—he'd robbed five hundred men of more than half an hour of their time.

The Moldavian hunched his shoulders and scurried along like a mouse. A guard shouted "Halt!" and took his number. "K-460. Where were you?" He walked up to the man as he spoke, turning his rifle butt end forward.

There were shouts from the crowd: "Bastard!" "Dog's vomit!" "Rotten shit!"

But others quieted down as soon as the sergeant turned his rifle around.

The Moldavian said nothing, just lowered his head and backed away from the sergeant. The deputy foreman of Gang 32 stepped forward.

"The rotten bastard climbed up on the plasterers' scaffolding to hide from me, managed to get warm up there, and fell asleep."

He gave the man a kidney punch. And a rabbit punch.

That way he sent him staggering out of the sergeant's reach.

But as the man reeled back a Hungarian belonging to the same gang, 32, sprang forward, kicked his behind, and kicked it again. (Hungarians don't like Romanians at the best of times.)

A bit different from spying, eh? Any idiot can be a spy. Spies live in comfort, spies have fun. You won't find a tenner on general duties in a hard-labor camp quite so easy.

The sergeant lowered his rifle.

"Get away from the gates! Form up in fives!" the guard commander yelled.

Counting again, the bastards! Why now, when they'd cleared it all up? An ugly noise went through the ranks. All the hatred they'd felt for the Moldavian was switched to the guards. They kept up their din and made no effort to move away from the gates.

"What's this, then?" the guard commander bellowed. "Want me to sit you down on the snow? Don't think I won't. I'll keep you here till morning!"

He would, too. Nothing out of the ordinary. Prisoners had been made to sit down often enough before. Or even lie down. It would be: "Down!

Guards—guns at the ready!" The zeks knew this sort of thing could happen. They started inching back from the gates.

The guards urged them on with shouts of "Get back! Get back there!"

Zeks in the rear shouted angrily at those in front. "What are you leaning on the gate for, anyway, you sons of bitches?" The mob was slowly forced backward.

"Form up in fives! First five! Second! Third!"

By now the moon was shining full-strength. The redness had gone and it had brightened up. It was a good quarter of the way up. The evening had gone to waste. Damn that Moldavian. Damn the guards. Damn this life of ours.

The front ranks, once counted, turned and stood on tiptoe, trying to see whether there'd be two men or three left in the rear. That was now a matter of life and death.

Shukhov thought for a moment there were going to be four. He felt weak with fright. One too many! another recount! But it turned out that Fetyukov, the scavenger, had gone to scrounge the captain's cigarette butt and hadn't got back to his place in time, so it looked as though there was one man extra.

The deputy guard commander lost his temper and punched Fetyukov in the neck.

Serve him right!

Now there were three in the rear rank. Got it right at last. Thank God for that!

"Get away from the gates!" The guards forced them back again.

This time the zeks didn't grumble. They could see soldiers coming out of the guardhouse and cordoning off a space on the other side of the gate.

Which meant that they would be allowed through.

The free overseers were nowhere to be seen, nor the site manager. The men would be getting their wood out.

The gates were flung wide. The guard commander and a checker were waiting once again by a log railing just outside.

"First five! Second! Third!"

If the numbers tallied this time, the sentries would be taken off the towers.

They had quite a long way to trudge around the boundary fence from the farthest towers. Only when the last zek was led out of the compound and the count came out right would the towers get a telephone call telling the guards to come down. Not a minute before. If the guard commander had any sense, he'd move out right away! He knew the zeks couldn't run for it, and he knew the men from the towers would catch up with the column. But a dim-witted commander might be afraid he wouldn't have men enough to handle the zeks, so he'd wait around.

Today's commander was one of those fatheads. He decided to wait.

The zeks had been out in the cold all day, almost frozen to death. And now they'd been standing freezing for a whole hour since quitting time. What really got them down, though, was not the cold but the maddening thought that their evening was ruined. There'd be no time for anything back in camp.

"How do you come to know so much about life in the British Navy?" somebody in the next rank was asking.

"Well, it's like this, I spent nearly a month on a British cruiser, had my own cabin. I was liaison officer with one of their convoys."

"That explains everything. Quite enough for them to pin twenty-five on you."

"Sorry, I don't go along with all that destructive liberal criticism. I think better of our legal system."

Bullshit, Shukhov said to himself (he didn't want to get involved). Senka Klevshin had been with the Americans for two days and he got nailed for twenty-five. You were sitting pretty on that ship of theirs for a month—how long does that entitle you to?

"Only, after the war the British admiral took it into his blasted head to send me a souvenir, a token of gratitude, he called it. What a nasty surprise, and how I cursed him for it!"

It was strange when you came to think of it. The bare steppe, the deserted site, the snow sparkling in the moonlight. The guards spaced out ten paces from each other, guns at the ready. The black herd of zeks. One of them, in the same sort of jacket as the rest, Shch-311, had never known life without golden epaulettes, had been pals with a British admiral, and here he was hauling a handbarrow with Fetyukov.

You can turn a man upside down, inside out, any way you like.

The guards were all there now, and it was "Quick march! Speed it up!" Just like that. No "prayers" this time.

Speed it up? The hell we will. No good hurrying now all the other work parties have gone on ahead. Without a word spoken, the zeks all had the same idea: you've held us up, now we'll hold you up. We know you're just as keen as we are to get in the warm.

"Step on it!" the guard commander shouted. "Front marker—step on it!" Like hell we will!

The zeks plodded on, heads down, like men going to a funeral. Nothing to lose now, we're last back in camp anyway. You wouldn't treat us like human beings, so bust a gut shouting.

The shouts—"Step on it!"—went on for a while, till the guard commander realized that the zeks wouldn't go any faster. Shooting was out of the question: they were walking in column, in ranks of five, in good order. There was nothing the guard commander could do to make them move more quickly. (In the morning the zeks' only hope of salvation is ambling to work slowly. Move briskly and you'll never finish your time—you'll run out of steam and collapse.)

They went on steadily, holding themselves back. Crunching through the snow. Some chatting quietly, some not bothering. Shukhov was trying to remember what he'd left undone in camp that morning. Oh, yes—the sick bay! Funny, that—he'd forgotten all about it while he was working.

They'd be seeing patients in the sick bay right now. He might still be in time if he skipped supper. But he didn't have much of an ache anymore. They wouldn't even take his temperature. Just a waste of time. He'd got by without doctors so far. And that lot could doctor you right into your coffin.

Supper, not the sick bay, was more attractive right now. How to manage a bit extra? The only hope was that Tsezar would get a parcel, it was high time he did.

A change suddenly came over the column of zeks. It wavered, stumbled, shuddered, muttered, and all at once the fives at the rear, Shukhov among them, were running to keep pace with those in front.

They would walk a few paces—and start running again.

When the tail end reached the hilltop Shukhov saw to their right, some distance away on the steppe, another black column on the move. The others must have spotted this column and speeded up to cut across its path.

It could only be the party from the engineering works—three hundred men. They, too, must have been unlucky enough to be kept behind. Shukhov wondered why. Sometimes they were kept back for work reasons— to finish repairing some machine or other. Didn't matter a lot to them, they were in the warm all day.

Now it was devil take the hindmost. The men were running, really running. The guards, too, broke into a trot, with the guard commander shouting: "Don't get strung out too far! Close up at the back there! Close up!"

Stop your yelping, God damn it! We *are* closing up, what do you think we're doing?

Whatever they'd been talking or thinking about was forgotten. The whole column had one thing and one thing only on its mind.

"Get ahead of Ten! Beat them to it!"

Things were all mixed up. No more sweet or sour. No more guard or zek. Guards and zeks were friends. The other column was the enemy.

Their spirits rose. Their anger vanished.

"Hurry it up! Get a move on!" the rear ranks shouted to those ahead.

Shukhov's column burst into the settlement and lost sight of the engineers beyond the houses. Now they were racing blind. Shukhov's column had better footing, in the middle of the road. And the guards at the sides of the street stumbled less. Now, if ever, was the time to squeeze the others out!

There was another good reason for getting in front of the engineers—it took longer to search them at the guardhouses. Since throat-cutting had broken out in the camp, the bosses reckoned that the knives must be made at the engineering works and smuggled in. So the engineers were frisked with extra care as they entered the camp. In late autumn, with the ground already chilly, the shout would go up: "Shoes off, engineers! Hold your shoes in your hands!"

And they were frisked barefoot.

Even now, frost or no frost, the guards would pick on somebody at random: "You there, off with your right boot! You over there—left one off!"

The zek would simply have to hop on the other foot while one boot was turned upside down and the foot rag shaken to make sure there was no knife.

Shukhov had heard—he didn't know whether it was true or not—that the engineers had brought two volleyball posts into the camp that summer, with all the knives hidden inside them. Ten big knives in each. One or two had been found lying around.

Half running, they passed the new recreation center, the free workers' houses, the woodworking plant, and pushed on to the turn toward the guardhouse.

"Hoo-oo-oo-oo-oo!" the column cried with a single voice.

That road junction was their goal. The engineers, a hundred and fifty meters to the right, had fallen behind.

They could take it easy now. The whole column rejoiced. Like rabbits finding that frogs, say, are afraid even of them.

And there it was—the camp. Just as they had left it. Darkness, lights over the tight fence around the compound, a dense battery of lamps blazing in front of the guardhouse, the search area flooded with what could have been sunlight.

But before they reached the guardhouse, the guard commander shouted, "Halt!"

He handed his submachine gun to a soldier and ran over to the column (they're told not to get too close together with their guns in hand).

"Those on the right carrying wood—drop it on the right!"

Those on the outside, where he could see them, didn't try to hide their wood. One bundle flew through the air, a second, a third. Some tried to hide their wood inside the column, but their neighbors turned on them.

"You'll make them take everybody else's! Chuck it down like a good boy!"

Who is the convict's worst enemy? Another convict. If zeks didn't squabble among themselves, the bosses would have no power over them.

"Quick—ma-arch!" the second-in-command shouted.

And they made for the guardhouse.

Five roads met at the guardhouse and an hour earlier they had all been crowded with prisoners from other work sites. If someday those roads became streets lined with buildings, the future civic center would surely be where the guardhouse and the frisking area now were. And where work parties now pressed in from all sides, parades would converge on public holidays.

The warders were there waiting, warming themselves in the guardhouse. They came out and formed up across the road.

"Undo your jackets! Undo your jerkins!"

Warders' arms wide open. Ready to embrace and frisk. Ready to slap each man's sides. Same as in the morning, more or less.

Unbuttoning wasn't too terrible now they were nearly home.

Yes—that's what they all called it, "home."

Their days were too full to remember any other home.

After they'd frisked the head of the column, Shukhov went up to Tsezar and said, "Tsezar Markovich! When we get past the guardhouse, I'll run and line up at the parcel room."

Tsezar turned his heavy black mustache (white now at the bottom) in Shukhov's direction.

"What's the point, Ivan Denisovich? There may not be a parcel."

"So what have I got to lose? I'll wait ten minutes, and if you don't come, I'll get back to the hut." (Thinking to himself, If Tsezar doesn't come, some-body else may, and I can sell him my place in the line.)

But it looked like Tsezar wanted that parcel pretty badly.

"All right, then," he said, "run and get a place, Ivan Denisovich. But don't stay more than ten minutes."

The search was getting closer. Shukhov moved along without fear. He had nothing to hide this time. He took his time unbuttoning his jacket, and loosened the canvas belt around his jerkin.

He hadn't remembered having anything forbidden, but wariness had become second nature after eight years inside. So he plunged his hand into the sewn-on pocket to make sure that it was empty—though he knew very well that it was.

Ah, but there was the little bit of broken blade! The one he'd picked up at the work site that morning, not wanting to see it wasted, but hadn't meant to bring into the camp.

He hadn't meant to—but now that he had brought it, it would be a ter-rible pity to throw the thing away. You could hone it in a nice little knife—shoemaker's or tailor's type, whichever you wanted.

If he'd thought of carrying it in, he'd also have thought up some good way of hiding it. There were only two ranks in front of him—and now the first of those peeled off and went to be frisked.

He had to decide quick as a flash whether to use the cover of the rank in front and drop the blade on the snow while nobody was looking (it would be found afterward, but they wouldn't know whose it was), or to keep it.

That bit of steel could cost him ten days in the hole if they decided it was a knife.

But a cobbler's knife was an earner, it meant extra bread!

Pity to throw it away.

Shukhov slipped it into his padded mitten.

The next five were ordered to step forward for frisking.

That left the last three men in the full glare of the lights: Senka, Shukhov, and the fellow from Gang 32 who had run after the Moldavian.

Just the three of them, and five warders stood facing them. So Shukhov could play it smart and choose which of the two warders on the right to approach. He ignored the young one with a high flush and chose the older man with a gray mustache. He was more experienced, of course, and could easily have found the blade if he had wanted to, but at his age he must hate the job like poison.

He'd taken off both mittens and was clutching them in one hand, with the empty one sticking out. He grasped the rope girdle in the same hand, unbuttoned his jerkin completely, obligingly plucked up the skirts of jacket and jerkin—he had never been so forthcoming at the search point before, but he wanted to show that he had nothing to hide—and at the command went up to Gray Whiskers.

The gray one patted Shukhov's sides and back, tapped the sewn-on pocket from outside—nothing there—fingered the skirts of the jerkin and jacket, gave a farewell squeeze to the mitten Shukhov was holding out, and found it empty . . .

When the warder squeezed his mitten, Shukhov felt as if somebody had his guts between pincers. A squeeze like that on the other mitten and he'd be done for—into the hole, on three hundred grams a day, no hot food for two days at a time. He imagined himself getting weaker and weaker from hunger, and thought how hard it would be to get back to his present wiry (not too well fed, but not starving) condition.

And he offered up a silent agonized prayer: "Save me, Lord! Don't let them put me in the hole!"

All these thoughts passed through his head while the warder was feeling the first mitten and letting his hand stray to the one behind it (he would have felt both at once, if Shukhov had held one in each hand). But at that very moment they heard the warder in charge of the search, in a hurry to get off-duty, call out to the guards:

"Bring up the engineers!"

So the gray-mustached warder, instead of tackling Shukhov's other mitten, waved him through. Scot-free.

Shukhov ran to catch up with his teammates. They were already drawn up in fives between the two long log rails that looked like the hitching place at a country market and formed a sort of paddock for the column. He ran lightly, no longer feeling the ground under his feet, forgetting to say another prayer, of gratitude this time, because he was in too much of a hurry, and anyway there was no point in it now.

The guards who had marched Shukhov's column in had now all moved over to make way for the engineers' guards and were only awaiting their commander. The wood dropped by the column before the frisk had been picked up by the convoy guards, while that confiscated by the warders during the search was piled up by the guardhouse.

The moon was sailing higher and higher and the frost was tightening its grip in the bright snowy night.

The guard commander, who had gone to the guardhouse to recover his receipt for 463 men, had a word with Pryakha, Volkovoy's second-in-command, who called out, "K-460."

The Moldavian, who had buried himself in the depths of the column, heaved a sigh and went over to the right-hand hitching rail. He kept his head down and his shoulders hunched.

"Over here!" Pryakha's finger showed him the way around the hitching rail.

The Moldavian went. He was ordered to put his hands behind his back and stand still.

So they meant to pin a charge of attempted escape on him. He'd be slung in the camp jail.

Two sentries took their stand to the right and left behind the paddock and just short of the gates. The gates, three times the height of a man, opened slowly, and the order rang out:

"Form up in fives!" (No need for "Get away from the gates" this time: camp gates always open inward, so if the zeks should mob them from inside they can't unhinge them.)

"Number One! Two! Three!"

Standing there to be counted through the gate of an evening, back in camp after a whole day of buffeting wind, freezing cold, and an empty belly, the zek longs for his ladleful of scalding-hot watery evening soup as for rain in time of drought. He could knock it back in a single gulp. For the moment that ladleful means more to him than freedom, more than his whole past life, more than whatever life is left to him.

The zeks go in through the camp gates like warriors returning from a campaign—blustering, clattering, swaggering: "Make way there, can't you!"

The trusty looking at the wave of returning zeks through the staff-hut window feels afraid.

After the evening count, the zek is a free man again for the first time since roll call at 6:30 in the morning. Through the great camp gates, through the smaller gates to the inner compound, along the midway between another pair of "hitching rails"—and every man could go his own way.

But not the foremen. A work assigner rounds them up with shouts of "Foremen! To the PPS!"

To try on tomorrow's horse collar.

Shukhov hurtled past the jailhouse, between the huts, and into the parcel room. While Tsezar, preserving his dignity, walked at a leisurely pace in the other direction, to where there was already a buzzing swarm of zeks around a plywood board nailed to a post and bearing the names written in indelible pencil of those who had parcels waiting for them.

They generally write on plywood, not paper, in the camps. It's tougher and more reliable. The screws and the work assigners jot down their head counts on plywood. You can scrape the figures off next day and use it again. Quite economical.

Another chance here for those left behind in camp to toady: they read on the board the name of a man who's got a parcel, meet him out on the midway, and tell him the number. It's not worth a lot—but even that may earn you the odd cigarette.

Shukhov ran to the parcel room—a lean-to built onto one of the huts, with a lobby tacked onto it. The lobby had no outer door, and the cold was free to enter—but it was still somehow cozier than outside. At least it had a roof.

The queue was all around the lobby wall. Shukhov got in line. There were at least fifteen in front of him. More than an hour's wait, which would take him exactly to lights-out. Those from the Power Station column who'd gone to look at the list would be behind him. So would the engineers. They might have to come back first thing in the morning.

The men on line had bags and sacks. On the other side of the door (Shukhov had heard said—he had never himself received a parcel in this camp) they opened the regulation boxes with a hatchet and a warder took every article out with his own hands, cutting it up, breaking it in two, prodding it or pouring it out to examine it. Jars or cans containing liquid would be broached and emptied—all you'd get was what you caught in your hands or netted in a towel. For some reason they were afraid to hand over the containers. If there was any sort of pie or cake, any unusual sweet, any sausage or smoked fish, the warder would take a bite. (Start demanding your rights and he'd give you the treatment—this forbidden, that isn't allowed—and you'd end up with nothing. Whoever gets a parcel has to give and keep on giving—the warder's only the beginning.) When they've finished searching, they still won't give you the box it came in—just sweep the lot into a bag, or the skirts of your jacket, and clear off. Next, please. They can hurry a man up so much he leaves something on the counter. He needn't bother going back. It won't be there.

Shukhov had received a couple of parcels back in Ust-Izhma, but he'd written to his wife not to send any more, not to rob the kids, it only went to waste.

It had been easier for Shukhov to feed his whole family as a free man than it was to feed just himself in the camps, but he knew what those parcels cost, and you couldn't go on milking your family for ten years on end. Better to do without.

That's what he'd decided, but whenever anybody in the gang or the hut got a parcel (somebody did almost every day) he felt a pang—why isn't it for me? And although he had strictly forbidden his wife to send anything even at Easter, and never went to look at the list on the post—except for some rich workmate—he sometimes found himself expecting somebody to come running and say:

"Why don't you go and get it, Shukhov? There's a parcel for you."

Nobody came running.

As time went by, he had less and less to remind him of the village of Temgenyovo and his cottage home. Life in camp kept him on the go from getting-up time to lights-out. No time for brooding on the past.

Standing among men who were savoring already the fatback they'd shortly sink their teeth into, the butter they'd smear on their bread, the sugar they'd sweeten their tea with, Shukhov's mind ran on one single desire—that he and his gang would get into the mess hut in time to eat their skilly hot. Cold, it wasn't worth half as much.

He reckoned that if Tsezar hadn't found his name on the list he'd have been back in the hut washing himself long ago. If his name was there, he'd be collecting sacks, plastic mugs, and wrapping paper. That was why Shukhov had promised to wait ten minutes.

Standing in the line, he heard a piece of news. No Sunday off this week, they were being cheated out of Sunday again. Just what he, and everybody else, had expected. If there were five Sundays in a month, they were allowed three and hustled off to work on the other two. He'd expected it, all right, but hearing it nevertheless cut him to the quick. Who wouldn't be sorry for his precious Sunday rest? Of course, what they were saying in the queue was true enough: your day off could be hell even in camp, they could always think up something for you to do, build a bit on to the bathhouse, or wall up a passage between huts, or tidy up the yard. Then there was changing mattresses, shaking them, and squashing the bugs in the bunks. Or else they could take it into their heads to check the description in your dossier. Or else there was stock-taking: get all your belongings out in the yard and sit there half the day.

Nothing seemed to upset them more than a zek sleeping after breakfast.

The line moved forward, slowly but steadily. Some people went inside, out of turn, shoving past the man at the head of the queue without a by-your-leave. The barber for one, and a bookkeeper, and a man from the CES. These weren't common or garden zeks but well-fixed trusties, the lousiest bastards of the lot, who spent all their time in camp. The working zeks regarded these people as utter shits (and *they* thought the same of the zeks). But it was useless to pick a quarrel with them: the trusties were all in cahoots with each other, and with the warders, too.

Anyway, there were still ten men in front of Shukhov, and another seven had fallen in behind, when Tsezar, wearing the new fur hat somebody had sent him from outside, came in through the opening, ducking his head. (Really something, that hat. Tsezar had greased somebody's palm, and gotten permission to wear it—a neat new town hat. Other people had even their shabby old army caps snatched from them, and were given ratty camp-issue caps instead.)

Tsezar smiled at Shukhov and got talking to an odd-looking fellow in glasses who'd been reading a newspaper all the time he was in the line.

"Aha! Pyotr Mikhailych!"

They opened up for each other like poppies in bloom.

"Look, I've got a recent *Evening Moscow*. Sent in a wrapper," the odd fellow said.

"Have you now!" Tsezar stuck his nose into the same paper. The bulb hanging from the ceiling was as dim as dim—how could they make anything out in that small print?

"There's a most interesting review of Zavadsky's premiere!"

These Muscovites could scent each other a long way off, like dogs. And when they got together they had their own way of sniffing each other all over. And they gabbled ever so fast, seeing who could get the most words in. And when they were at it there'd only be the odd Russian word—it was like listening to Latvians or Romanians.

Anyway, Tsezar had all his bags ready.

"So, I'll er . . . be off now, Tsezar Markovich," Shukhov lisped.

Tsezar raised his black mustache from the newspapers. "Of course, of course. Let's see, now, who's ahead of me? Who's behind me?"

Shukhov carefully explained who was where, and, without waiting for Tsezar to mention it, asked: "Shall I fetch your supper for you?"

(Meaning bring it in a mess tin from the mess hall to the hut. It was strictly forbidden, and any number of orders had been issued on the subject. If you were caught the mess tin was emptied on the ground and you were put in the hole—but people went on doing it, and always would, because a man with jobs to do would never get to the mess hut on time with his own gang.)

Shukhov's real thought was "You'll let me have your supper, won't you? You wouldn't be that stingy! You know there's no gruel at suppertime, just skilly without trimmings."

Tsezar gave him a little smile. "No, no, eat it yourself, Ivan Denisovich."

That was all he was waiting for. He fluttered out of the anteroom like an uncaged bird and was off across the compound as fast as he could go.

Zeks were dashing around all over the place! At one time the camp commandant had given orders that zeks were not to walk about the camp singly. Whenever possible, they should be marched in gangs. And where it was quite impossible for a whole gang to go together—to sick bay, say, or the latrine—a group of four or five should be made up and one man put in charge to march them there, wait, and march them back again.

The commandant set great store by that order. Nobody dared argue with him. The warders grabbed lone wanderers, took down their numbers, hauled them off to the jailhouse—but in the end the order was ditched. Quietly—as so many loudmouthed orders are. Suppose they themselves wanted to call somebody in to see the godfather—they weren't going to send an escort party with him! Or suppose one man wanted to collect his food supply from the storeroom—why should another man have to go with him? Or say somebody took it into his head to go and read the papers in the CES—who on earth would want to go with him? One man has to take his boots to be mended, another is off to the drying room, somebody else just wants to wander from hut to hut (that's more strictly forbidden than anything else!)—how are you going to stop them?

The fat pig was trying to deprive the zek of the last scrap of liberty remaining to him. But it didn't work.

Meeting a warder on the way, and raising his cap to him just to be on the safe side, Shukhov ran into the hut. Inside, there was uproar: somebody's rations had been rustled during the day. Men were shouting at the orderlies, and they were shouting back. But 104's corner was empty.

Shukhov's idea of a happy evening was when they got back to the hut and didn't find the mattresses turned upside down after a daytime search.

He rushed to his bed place, shrugging off his jacket on the way. Up went his jacket, up went the mittens with the bit of metal in one of them, deep into the mattress went his fumbling hand—and his bread was still where he had put it that morning! Lucky he'd sewn it in!

Outside at a trot! To the mess hut!

He dashed to the mess without bumping into a warder. Only zeks wandered across his path, arguing about rations.

Outside, under the bright moon, it was getting lighter all the time. All the lamps were dim, and the huts cast black shadows. The entrance to the mess hut was up four steps and across a wide porch, also now in the shadows. But a little lamp swayed above it, squeaking in the cold. Frost, or dirt, gave every light bulb a rainbow-colored halo.

Another of the commandant's strict orders was that the gangs should go in two at a time. On reaching the mess, the order went on to say, gangs should not mount the steps but re-form in ranks of five and stand still until the mess orderly let them in.

Limpy had hooked the mess orderly's job and held on to it for dear life. He'd promoted his limp to a disability but the bastard was fighting fit. He'd found himself a birch thumb stick and stood on the porch using it to pin back anybody who started up the steps before he gave the order. Well, not everybody. Limpy had a quick eye and knew who was who even in the shadows and from the rear. He wasn't going to strike anybody who might give him a smack in the kisser. He only beat those who'd been beaten into shape for him. He'd nailed Shukhov once.

"Orderly" he was called. But when you thought of it, he was a prince. The cooks were his pals!

This time, whether because the gangs had all rolled up at once, or because it had taken so long to get things sorted out, a dense crowd swarmed around the porch, with Limpy, his stooge, and the mess manager up above. The sons of bitches could do without warders.

The mess manager was an overstuffed swine with a head like a pumpkin and shoulders a yard and a half across. He was so strong he looked fit to burst, and walked in jerks as though his legs and arms had springs instead of joints. He wore a white fur hat, without a number patch. Not one of the free workers had a hat like that. He also wore an Astrakhan waistcoat, with a little number patch no bigger than a postage stamp on his chest—to humor Volkovoy. There wasn't even a patch of that size on his back. The mess manager bowed to nobody, and the zeks were all afraid of him. He held thousands of lives in one hand! He nearly got beaten up once but the cooks all rushed to the rescue—and what a bunch of thugs they were!

It would be a disaster if 104 had gone through already. Limpy knew the whole camp by sight, and with the mess manager there, he wouldn't let you past with the wrong gang. He'd be looking for somebody to make a monkey of.

Prisoners sometimes sneaked over the porch rails behind Limpy's back. Shukhov had done it himself. But, with the manager there, you couldn't do it—he'd bounce you so hard you'd just about make it to sick bay.

Quick now, up to the porch and try and find out in the dark whether 104 are among that mass of identical black coats.

Just then the gangs began heaving and shoving (nothing else for it—lights-out soon!), as though they were storming a fortress, taking the steps one at a time and swarming onto the porch.

"Halt, you sons of bitches!" Limpy roared, raising his stick at those in front. "I'll split somebody's head open in a minute!"

"We can't help it!" those in front yelled in reply. "They're shoving from behind."

The shoving was coming from behind, all right, but the front rows were hoping to go flying through the mess-hut door and didn't put up much resistance.

Limpy held his staff across his chest like the barrier at a level crossing and charged the front rank full-tilt. His stooge also gripped the staff, and even the mess manager wasn't too proud to soil his hands on it.

They were pushing downhill, and they were stronger—they got meat to eat—so the zeks gave ground. The front rank reeled back down the steps onto those behind them and they in turn onto those still farther back, toppling them over like sheaves.

Some of the crowd yelled, . . . but they took care not to be spotted. The rest collapsed in silence, and rose in silence, quick as they could, before they were trampled.

The steps were cleared. The mess manager withdrew along the porch, and Limpy stood on the top step, laying down the law:

"Sort yourselves out in fives, you blockheads, how many more times do I have to tell you? I'll let you in when I'm good and ready!"

Shukhov was so happy it hurt when he spotted what looked like Senka Klevshin's head right up by the porch. He set his elbows to work as fast as they'd go, but there was no breaking through that solid wall of backs.

"Gang 27!" Limpy shouted. "In you go!"

Gang 27 hopped onto the porch and rushed for the door. The rest surged up the steps in their wake, pushed from behind. Shukhov was one of those shoving with all his might. The porch shook and the lamp above it was squeaking.

Limpy flared up. "At it again, you scum?" His stick played on backs and shoulders and men were knocked flying into those behind.

The steps were clear again.

From down below, Shukhov saw Pavlo up beside Limpy. Pavlo always led the gang to the mess, Tyurin wouldn't rub shoulders with a mob like this.

"104, form up in fives," Pavlo shouted down at them. "And you make way there, friends!"

The friends would be hanged first.

Shukhov shook the man in front. "You with your back to me, let me through! That's my gang."

The man would have been glad to let him through, but was wedged in himself.

The crowd swayed, risking suffocation for the sake of its skilly, its lawful entitlement of skilly.

Shukhov tried something else: he grabbed the rails to his left, shifted his hold to the post supporting the porch, and took off from the ground. His feet bumped against somebody's knees, he collected a few punches in the ribs and a few foul names, but then he was in the clear: standing on the top step, with one foot on the porch. His teammates spotted him and reached out to help him.

The mess manager, leaving the porch, looked around from the door.

"Two more gangs, Limpy."

"104!" Limpy shouted. "Where do you think you're going, scum?" He brought his staff down on an intruder's neck.

"104!" Pavlo shouted, letting his men through.

"Phew!" Shukhov burst into the mess. And was off, looking for empty trays, without waiting for Pavlo to tell him.

The mess was its usual self—frosty air steaming in from the door, men at the tables packed as tight as seeds in a sunflower, men wandering between tables, men trying to barge their way through with full trays. But Shukhov was used to all this after so many years, and his sharp eye saw something else: Shch-208 was carrying only five bowls, so that must be his gang's last tray, otherwise it would be a full one.

Shukhov, behind him, slipped the words into his ear: "I'll come and get the tray, pal—I'm right behind you."

"That fellow over by the window's waiting for it, I promised him . . ."

"He can take a running jump—should've kept his eyes open."

They made a deal.

Shch-208 carried his tray to the table and unloaded it. When Shukhov grabbed it, the other man, the one who'd been promised, rushed over and started tugging at the other side. He was a weakling compared with Shukhov, though. Shukhov pushed the tray at him as he pulled, he reeled back against a roof support, and the tray was wrenched from his hands. Shukhov tucked it under his arm and trotted off to the serving hatch.

Pavlo, standing in line there, dismally waiting for trays, was overjoyed to see him.

"Ivan Denisovich!" He pushed past the deputy foreman of Gang 27. "Let me through! No good you standing there! I've got trays!"

Sure enough, Gopchik, the little scamp, was lugging another one over.

"They took their eyes off it, so I nicked it," he said with a laugh.

Gopchik had the makings of a really good camp dweller. Give him another three years, let him grow up a bit, and fate had something good in store for him—a bread cutter's job at least.

Pavlo ordered Yermolaev, the tough Siberian (another ex-POW doing ten), to take the second tray and sent Gopchik to look for a table where supper was nearly over. Shukhov rested one corner of his tray on the counter and waited.

"104!" Pavlo announced through the hatch.

There were five hatches altogether: three to serve ordinary prisoners, one for those on special diet (a dozen with stomach ulcers, and all the bookkeepers for a kickback), and one for the return of dirty bowls (with people around it fighting to lick them). The counters were not much more than waist-high. The cooks couldn't be seen through the hatches, only their hands and ladles.

This cook's hands were white and well manicured, but strong and hairy. A boxer's hands, not a cook's. He took a pencil and ticked off something on a list pinned up behind the partition.

"104—twenty-four."

So Panteleyev had crawled over to the mess. Not ill at all, the son of a bitch.

The cook picked up a huge ladle, a three-liter one, and stirred the pail busily. (It had just been refilled, almost to the top, and steam billowed out of it.) Then he grabbed a smaller, 750-gram ladle and began dishing out the skilly, without dipping very deep.

"One, two, three, four . . ."

Shukhov took note which dishes had been filled before the solids had sunk to the bottom of the pail, and which held thin stuff, nothing but water. He lined up ten bowls on his tray and carried it off. Gopchik was waving to him from near the second row of pillars.

"Over here, Ivan Denisovich, over here!"

Carrying a tray laden with bowls is not as easy as it looks. Shukhov glided along, taking care not to jolt the tray, and leaving the hard work to his vocal cords.

"Hey, you, Kh-920! Look out, man! . . . Out of the way there, lad!"

In a crush like that, it's a tricky business carrying just one bowl to the table without spilling it, and Shukhov had ten of them. All the same, there were no fresh splashes on the tray when he set it down gently on the end of the table liberated by Gopchik. He even skillfully turned the tray so that he would be sitting at the corner with the two bowls of really thick skilly.

Yermolaev arrived with another ten bowls, and Gopchik and Pavlo hurried over with the last four in their hands.

Kildigs came next, with some bread on a tray. Food today was according to the amount of work done—some had earned two hundred grams, some three hundred, and Shukhov four hundred. He took his four hundred—a big crust—and two hundred grams from the middle of the loaf, which was Tsezar's ration.

The gang trickled in from all over the mess to take their supper away and lap it up wherever they could sit. Shukhov handed out the bowls, ticking off each man as he collected, and keeping an eye on his own corner of the tray. He had slipped his spoon into one of the bowls of thick skilly to show that it was taken. Fetyukov was one of the first to pick up a bowl. He carried it off, realizing that there would be slim pickings in his own gang today and that he might have more luck scavenging around the mess. Somebody might leave a spot. (Whenever a man pushed his bowl away without emptying it, others swooped like birds of prey, sometimes several at once.)

Shukhov and Pavlo counted up the portions. It looked about right. Shukhov slipped Pavlo a bowl of the thick stuff for Andrei Prokofyevich, and Pavlo poured it into a narrow German flask with a lid. He could carry it out hugged to his chest under his coat.

They turned in their trays. Pavlo sat down to his double portion, and Shukhov to his two bowls. No more talk. The sacred minutes had arrived.

Shukhov took off his cap and put it on his knees. He checked one bowl, then the other, with his spoon. Not too bad, there was even a bit of fish. The skilly was always a lot thinner in the evening than in the morning: a zek had to be fed in the morning so that he could work, but in the evening he'd sleep, hungry or not, and wouldn't croak overnight.

He began eating. First he just drank the juice, spoon after spoon. The warmth spread through his body, his insides greeted that skilly with a joyful fluttering. This was it! This was good! This was the brief moment for which a zek lives.

For a little while Shukhov forgot all his grievances, forgot that his sentence was long, that the day was long, that once again there would be no Sunday. For the moment he had only one thought: We shall survive. We shall survive it all. God willing, we'll see the end of it!

When he had sucked up the hot juice from both bowls, he emptied what was left in one into the other—tipping it up and then scraping it clean with his spoon. He would feel easier not having to think about the second bowl, not having to guard it with his eyes or his hand.

Now that his eyes were off-duty, he shot a glance at his neighbor's bowls. The man to his left had nothing but water. Dirty dogs—treating fellow zeks like that!

Now Shukhov was eating cabbage with the remains of his slop. The two bowls between them had caught a single potato—in Tsezar's bowl it was. An average-sized potato, frostbitten of course, sweetish, and with hard bits in it. There was hardly any fish at all, just an occasional glimpse of a boiled-bare backbone. Still, every bone and every fin had to be thoroughly chewed, and the juice sucked out of them—the juice did you good. All this, of course, took time, but Shukhov was in no hurry. Today was a holiday for him: he'd lifted two portions for dinner and two for supper. Any other business could be put off while he dealt with this.

Though maybe he ought to call on the Latvian for his tobacco. There might be none left by morning.

Shukhov was eating his supper without bread: two portions with bread as well would be a bit too rich. The bread would come in useful tomorrow. The belly is an ungrateful wretch, it never remembers past favors, it always wants more tomorrow.

Shukhov finished off his skilly, not taking much notice of those around him—it didn't much matter, he was content with his lawful portion and had no hankering after anything more. All the same, he did notice the tall old man, Yu-81, sit down opposite him when the place became free. Shukhov knew that he belonged to Gang 64, and standing in line in the parcel room he'd heard that 64 had been sent to Sotsgorodok in place of 104, and spent the whole day stringing up barbed wire—making themselves a compound—with nowhere to get warm.

He'd heard that this old man had been in prison time out of mind—in fact, as long as the Soviet state had existed; that all the amnesties had passed him by, and that as soon as he finished one tenner they'd pinned another on him.

This was Shukhov's chance to take a close look at him. With hunched-over lags all round, he was as straightbacked as could be. He sat tall, as though he'd put something on the bench under him. That head hadn't needed a barber for ages: the life of luxury had caused all his hair to fall out. The old man's eyes didn't dart around to take in whatever was going on in the mess, but stared blindly at something over Shukhov's head. He was steadily eating his thin skilly, but instead of almost dipping his head in the bowl like the rest of them, he carried his battered wooden spoon up high. He had no teeth left, upper or lower, but his bony gums chewed his bread just as well without them. His face was worn thin, but it wasn't the weak face of a burnt-out invalid, it was like dark chiseled stone. You could tell from his big chapped and blackened hands that in all his years inside he'd never had a soft job as a trusty. But he refused to knuckle under: he didn't put his three hundred grams on the dirty table, splashed all over, like the others, he put it on a rag he washed regularly.

No time to go on studying him, though. Shukhov licked his spoon and tucked it inside his boot, crammed his cap on his head, rose, picked up the bread—his own ration and Tsezar's—and left. You went out by the back porch, past two orderlies with nothing to do other than lift the catch, let you out, and lower the catch again.

Shukhov left with a well-filled belly, at peace with himself, and decided to pop over to the Latvian even though it was nearly lights-out. He strode briskly toward Hut 7, without stopping to leave the bread at No. 9.

The moon was as high as it would ever be, it looked like a hole cut in the sky. The sky was cloudless. With here and there the brightest stars you ever saw. But Shukhov had less time still for studying the sky. All he knew was that the frost wasn't easing up. Somebody had heard from the free workers—it had been on the radio—that they were expecting thirty degrees below at night and forty by morning.

You could hear things a long way off. A tractor roaring in the settlement. The grating noise of an excavator over toward the highroad. The crunch of every pair of felt boots walking or running across the camp.

There was no wind now.

He was going to buy homegrown tobacco at the same price as before—a ruble for a tumblerful. Outside the camp, it cost three rubles, or more, depending on the quality. But prices in the camps weren't like those anywhere else. You weren't allowed to hang on to money, so what little you had bought more. This camp paid no money wage.[21] (In Ust-Izhma, Shukhov had earned thirty rubles a month—better than nothing.) If a man's family sent him money, it wasn't passed on to him but credited to his personal account. This credit gave him the right to buy toilet soap, moldy gingerbread, and Prima cigarettes once a month in the camp shop. Whether you liked them or not, you had to buy the goods once you'd ordered them through the commandant. If you didn't buy, the money was written off and you'd seen the last of it.

Money came Shukhov's way only from the private jobs he did: two rubles for making slippers from rags supplied by the customer, an agreed price for patching a jerkin.

Hut 7 wasn't divided into two large sections like No. 9. In Hut 7, ten doors opened onto a large corridor. Seven double-decker bunks were wedged into every room, and occupied by a single gang. There was also a cubicle below the night-tub storeroom, and another for the hut monitor. The artists had a cubicle as well.

Shukhov went into the room where his Latvian was. He was lying on the lower bed space with his feet up on the brace, gabbling away to his neighbor in Latvian.

Shukhov sat down by him, and mumbled some sort of greeting. The other man answered without lowering his feet. It was a small room, and they were all curious to know who this was and why he had come. Both of them realized this, so Shukhov sat there talking about nothing. How're you getting along, then? Not too bad. Cold today. Yes, it is.

He waited for the others to start talking again—they were arguing about the Korean War: would there be a world war now that the Chinese had joined in?—then bent his head toward the Latvian: "Any homegrown?"

"Yes."

---

21. Following Stalin's 1948 decision to establish separate ("special") camps for political offenders, money wages were paid only in the camps for common criminals.

"Let's have a look."

The Latvian swung his feet down from the angle brace, lowered them to the gangway, and rose. A skinflint, this Latvian—frightened to death he might stuff one smoke too many into the tumbler.

He showed Shukhov the pouch and snapped open the clasp.

Shukhov took a pinch on his palm and saw that it was the same as last time—same cut, and dark brown. He raised it to his nose and sniffed—yes, it was the same. But what he said to the Latvian was "Doesn't seem the same, somehow."

"It is! It is the same!" the Latvian said angrily. "I never have any other sort, it's always the same."

"All right, all right," Shukhov said agreeably. "Give me a good tumblerful and I'll try a puff. Maybe I'll take two lots."

He said, Give me a good tumblerful, because the Latvian always packed the tobacco loosely.

The Latvian took another pouch fatter than the first from under his pillow and got a beaker from his locker. A plastic one, but Shukhov had measured it and knew it held the same as a glass tumbler.

The Latvian shook tobacco into it.

"Come on, press it down a bit," Shukhov said, pushing his own finger into the beaker.

"I don't need your help." The Latvian snatched the beaker away angrily and pressed the tobacco down himself, but less firmly. He shook in some more.

In the meantime, Shukhov unbuttoned his jerkin and groped in the quilted lining for the bit of paper which only his fingers could feel. He used both hands to ease it gradually through the padding toward a little hole in quite a different part of the lining, loosely drawn together with two little stitches. When he had worked it as far as the hole, he pulled the stitches out with his fingernails, folded the piece of paper lengthwise yet again (it was already folded into a long, narrow strip), and drew it out. A two-ruble note. A well-worn one that didn't crackle.

Somebody in the room was bellowing: "Old Man Whiskers won't ever let you go! He wouldn't trust his own brother, let alone a bunch of cretins like you!"

The good thing about hard-labor camps is that you have all the freedom in the world to sound off. In Ust-Izhma you'd only have to whisper that people couldn't buy matches outside and they'd clap another ten on you. Here you could shout anything you liked from a top bunk and the stoolies wouldn't report it, because the security officer couldn't care less.

But Shukhov couldn't afford to hang around talking.

"It's still pretty loose," he complained.

"Here, then!" the other man said, adding an extra pinch.

Shukhov took his pouch from his inside pocket and tipped the home-grown into it from the beaker.

"Right," he said. He didn't want to rush off with his first sweet cigarette on the go. "Fill me another."

He haggled a bit more while the beaker was filled again, then handed his two rubles over, nodded to the Latvian, and went on his way.

Once outside, he was in a great hurry to reach his own hut. He didn't want to miss Tsezar when he got back with the parcel.

But Tsezar was there already, sitting on his lower bunk, feasting his eyes. He had arranged what he had brought on the bunk and on the nightstand. Both were screened from the lamp overhead by Shukhov's upper bunk, and it was pretty dark down there.

Shukhov bent over, inserted himself between Tsezar's bed space and the captain's, and held his hand out.

"Your bread, Tsezar Markovich."

He didn't say, "You got it, then"—that would have been a hint that he was entitled to a share for keeping Tsezar's place in the line. He knew his rights, of course. But even after eight years on general duties he was no scrounger, and as time went by, he was more and more determined not to be.

He couldn't control his eyes, though—the hawk eyes of an old camp hand. They skimmed over the contents of Tsezar's parcel laid out on the bed and the nightstand. The wrappings had not all been removed, and some bags had not been opened at all, but a quick glance and a sniff to make sure told Shukhov that Tsezar had been sent sausage, condensed milk, a big smoked fish, some fatback, biscuits with a nice smell, cake with a different nice smell, at least two kilos of lump sugar, and maybe some butter, as well as cigarettes, pipe tobacco, and quite a few other things.

He learned all this in the time it took to say: "Your bread, Tsezar Markovich."

Tsezar's eyes were wild and his hair all tousled. He was drunk with excitement. (People who received parcels of groceries always got into that state.) He waved the bread away: "Keep it, Ivan Denisovich."

The skilly, and two hundred grams of bread as well—that was a full supper, worth quite as much as Shukhov's share of Tsezar's parcel.

He immediately stopped expecting anything from the goodies on display. No good letting your belly get excited when there's nothing to come.

He'd got four hundred grams of bread, and another two hundred, and at least two hundred in his mattress. That was plenty. He could wolf down two hundred now, gobble up five hundred and fifty in the morning, and still have four hundred to take to work. He was really living it up! The bread in the mattress could stay there a bit. Good job he'd stitched the hole up in time. Somebody in Gang 75 had had things pinched from his nightstand.

(Ask the Supreme Soviet to look into it!)

Some people take the view that a man with a parcel is always a tightwad, you have to gouge what you can out of them. But when you think of it—it's easy come, easy go. Even those lucky people are sometimes glad to earn an extra bowl of gruel between parcels. Or scrounge a butt. A bit for the warder, a bit for the team foreman, and you can't leave out the trusty in the parcel room. If you do, he'll mislay your parcel next time around and it'll be there a week before it gets on the list. Then there's the clerk in the storeroom, where all the groceries have to be handed in—Tsezar will be taking a bagful there before work parade next morning to be kept safe from thieves, and hut searches, and because the commandant has so ordered—if you don't make the clerk a handsome gift, he'll pinch a bit here and a bit there . . . He sits there all day behind a locked door with other men's groceries, the rat, and there's no way of checking up on him. Then there's payment for services rendered (by Shukhov to Tsezar, for instance). Then there'll be a little something for the bathhouse man, so he'll pick you out a decent set of clean underwear. Then there's the barber, who shaves you "with paper"—wiping the razor on a scrap of paper, not your bare knee—it may not amount to much, but you have to give him three or four cigarettes. Then there'll be somebody in the CES—to make sure your letters are put aside separately and not lost. Then supposing you want to wangle a day off and rest up in the compound—you need to fix the doctor. You're bound to give something to your neighbor who eats from the same nightstand, like the captain does with Tsezar. And counts every bite you take. The most shameless zek can't hold out against that.

So those who always think the other man's radish is plumper than their own might feel envy, but Shukhov knew what was what and didn't let his belly rumble for other people's goodies.

By now he'd pulled his boots off, climbed up on his bunk, taken the fragment of steel out of his mitten, examined it, and made up his mind to look for a good stone next day and hone himself a cobbler's knife—work at it a bit morning and evening and in four days he'd have a great little knife with a sharp, curved blade.

For the time being, the steel had to be hidden, even at night. He could wedge it between his bedboards and one of the crossbars. While the captain wasn't there for the dust to fall in his face, Shukhov turned back his heavy mattress (stuffed with sawdust, not shavings) at the pillow end, and set about hiding the blade.

His neighbors up top—Alyoshka the Baptist and the two Estonian brothers on the next bunk across the gangway—could see him, but Shukhov knew he was safe with them.

Fetyukov passed down the hut, sobbing. He was bent double. His lips were smeared with blood. He must have been beaten up again for licking out bowls. He walked past the whole team without looking at anybody, not trying to hide his tears, climbed onto his bunk, and buried his face in his mattress.

You felt sorry for him, really. He wouldn't see his time out. He didn't know how to look after himself.

At that point the captain appeared, looking happy, carrying specially brewed tea in a mess tin. There were two buckets of tea in the hut, if you could call it tea. Warm and tea-colored, all right, but like dishwater. And the bucket made it smell of moldy wood pulp. Tea for the common working man, that was. Buynovsky must have gotten a handful of real tea from Tsezar, popped it in the mess tin, and fetched hot water from the boiler. He settled down at his nightstand, mighty pleased with himself.

"Nearly scalded my fingers under the tap," he said, showing off.

Down below there, Tsezar unfolded a sheet of paper and laid things out on it. Shukhov put his mattress back in place, so he wouldn't see and get upset. But yet again they couldn't manage without him. Tsezar rose to his full height in the gangway, so that his eyes were on a level with Shukhov's and winked: "Denisovich! Lend us your ten-day gadget."

The little folding knife, he meant. Shukhov had one hidden in his bed. Smaller than your finger crooked at the middle knuckle, but the devil would cut fatback five fingers thick. Shukhov had made a beautiful job of that knife and kept it well honed.

He felt for the knife, drew it out, and handed it over. Tsezar gave him a nod and vanished again.

The knife was another earner. Because you could land in the hole (ten days!) for keeping it. Only somebody with no conscience at all would say lend us your knife so we can cut our sausage, and don't think you're getting any.

Tsezar had put himself in debt to Shukhov again.

Now that he'd dealt with the bread and the knives, Shukhov fished out his pouch. He took from it a pinch exactly as big as that he had borrowed and held it out across the gangway to the Estonian, with a thank-you.

The Estonian's lips straightened into a smile of sorts, he muttered something to his brother, and they rolled a separate cigarette to sample Shukhov's tobacco.

Go ahead and try it, it's no worse than yours! Shukhov would have tried it himself, but the clock in his guts said it was very close to roll call. Just the time for the warders to come prowling round the huts. If he wanted a smoke he'd have to go out in the corridor quick, and he fancied it was a bit warmer up on his top bunk. It wasn't at all warm in the hut, and the ceiling was still patterned with hoarfrost. You'd get pretty chilly at night, but for the time being, it was just about bearable.

All his little jobs done, Shukhov began breaking bits from his two hundred grams. He couldn't help listening to the captain and Tsezar drinking tea and talking down below.

"Help yourself, Captain, don't be shy! Have some of this smoked fish. Have some sausage."

"Thank you, I will."

"Butter yourself a piece of this loaf! It's a real Moscow baton!"

"Dear-oh-dear-oh-dear, I just can't believe that somewhere or other batons are still being baked. This sudden abundance reminds me of something that once happened to me. It was at Sevastopol, before the Yalta Conference. The town was absolutely starving and we had to show an American admiral around. So they set up a shop specially, chockful of foodstuff, but it wasn't to be opened until they saw us half a block away, so that the locals wouldn't have time to crowd the place out. Even so, the shop was half full one minute after it opened. And you couldn't ask for the wrong thing. 'Look, butter!' people were shouting, 'Real butter! And white bread!'"

Two hundred harsh voices were raising a din in their half of the hut, but Shukhov still thought he could make out the clanging on the rail. Nobody else heard, though. Shukhov also noticed that the warder they called Snub Nose—a short, red-faced young man—had appeared in the hut. He was holding a piece of paper, and this and his whole manner showed that he hadn't come to catch people smoking or drive them outside for roll call, but was looking for somebody in particular.

Snub Nose consulted his piece of paper and asked: "Where's 104?"

"Here," they answered. The Estonians concealed their cigarettes and waved the smoke away.

"Where's the foreman?"

"What do you want?" Tyurin spoke from his bed, swinging his legs over the edge so that his feet barely touched the floor.

"Have the men who were told to submit written explanations got them ready?"

"They're doing it," Tyurin said confidently.

"They should have been in by now."

"Some of my men are more or less illiterate, it's hard work for them." (Tsezar and the captain, he was talking about. He was sharp, Tyurin. Never stuck for an answer.) "We've got no pens, or ink."

"Well, you should have."

"They keep confiscating it."

"Watch it, foreman, just mind what you're saying, or I'll have you in the cell block," Snub Nose promised, mildly. "The explanatory notes will be in the warders' barracks before work parade in the morning! And you will report that all prohibited articles have been handed in to the personal-property store. Understood?"

"Understood."

("The captain's in the clear!" Shukhov thought. The captain himself was purring over his sausage and didn't hear a thing.)

"Now, then," said the warder. "Shcha-301—is he in your gang?"

"I'll have to look at the list," the foreman said, pretending ignorance. "How can anybody be expected to remember these blasted numbers?" (If he could drag it out till roll call, he might save Buynovsky at least for the night.)

"Buynovsky—is he here?"

"Eh? That's me!" the captain piped up from his hiding place under Shukhov's top bunk.

The quick louse is always first on the comb.

"You, is it? Right then, Shcha-301. Get ready."

"To go where?"

"You know where."

The captain only sighed and groaned. Taking a squadron of torpedo boats out into a stormy sea in the pitch dark must have been easier for him than leaving his friends' company for the icy cell block.

"How many days?" he asked in a faint voice.

"Ten. Come along now, hurry it up!"

Just then the orderlies began yelling, "Roll call! Everybody out for roll call!"

The warder sent to call the roll must be in the hut already.

The captain looked back, wondering whether to take his overcoat. If he did, though, they'd whip it off him and leave him just his jerkin. So better go as he was. The captain had hoped for a while that Volkovoy would forget—but Volkovoy never forgot or forgave—and had made no preparations, hadn't even hidden himself a bit of tobacco in his jerkin. No good holding it in his hand—they'd take it off him the moment they frisked him.

All the same, Tsezar slipped him a couple of cigarettes while he was putting his cap on.

"Well, so long, chums," the captain said with a miserable look, nodding to his teammates, and followed the warder out of the hut.

Several voices called after him, "Keep smiling," "Don't let them get you down"—but there was nothing much you could say. Gang 104 had built the punishment block themselves and knew all about it: the walls were stone, the floor cement, there were no windows at all, the stove was kept just warm enough for the ice on the wall to melt and form puddles on the floor. You slept on bare boards, got three hundred grams of bread a day, skilly only every third day.

Ten days! Ten days in that cell block, if they were strict about and made you sit out the whole stint, meant your health was ruined for life. It meant tuberculosis and the rest of your days in the hospital.

Fifteen days in there and you'd be six feet under.

Thank heaven for your cozy hut, and keep your nose clean.

"Outside, I said—I'll count to three," the hut orderly shouted. "If any-body's not outside when I get to three, I'll take down his number and report him to the warder."

The hut orderly's another arch-bastard. Imagine—they lock him in with us for the whole night and he isn't afraid of anybody, because he's got the camp brass behind him. It's the other way around—everybody's afraid of him. He'll either betray you to the warders or punch you in the kisser. Disabled, supposed to be, because he lost a finger in a brawl, but he looks like a hood. And that's just what he is—convicted as a common criminal, but they pinned a charge under Article 58, subsection 14^{22} on him as well, which is why he landed in this camp.

There was nothing to stop him jotting your name down, handing it to the warder, and it was two days in the hole, normal working hours. Men had been drifting toward the door, but now they all crowded out, those on the top bunks flopping down like bears to join the milling crowd, trying to push their way through the narrow opening.

Shukhov sprang down nimbly, holding the cigarette he'd just rolled and had been wanting so long, thrust his feet into his boots and was ready to go—but he took pity on Tsezar. Not that he wanted to earn a bit more from Tsezar, he just pitied the man with all his heart: Tsezar might think a lot of himself, but he didn't know the first thing about the facts of life. When you got a parcel, you didn't sit gloating over it, you rushed it off to the storeroom before roll call. Eating could wait. But what could Tsezar do with his parcel now? If he turned out for roll call carrying that great big bag, what a laugh that would be—five hundred men would be roaring with laughter. If he left the stuff where it was, it would very likely be pinched by the first man back from roll call. (In Ust-Izhma the system was even tougher: the crooks would always be home from work first, and by the time the others got in, their nightstands would be cleaned out.)

Shukhov saw that Tsezar was in a panic—but he should have thought about it sooner. He was shoving the fatback and sausage under his shirt—if nothing else, he might be able to take them out to roll call and save them.

Shukhov took pity on him and told him how it was done:

"Sit tight, Tsezar Markovich—lie low, out of the light, and go out last. Don't stir till the warder and the orderlies come around the beds looking in every nook and cranny—then you can go out. Tell 'em you aren't well! And I'll go out first and hop back in first. That's the way to do it."

---

22. This section dealt with "counterrevolutionary sabotage" and could be applied to any action judged to have negative economic consequences.

And off he dashed.

He had to be pretty rough to start with, shoving his way through the crowd (taking good care, though, of the cigarette in his clenched hand). But there was no more shoving in the corridor shared by both halves of the hut and near the outer door. The crafty lot stuck like flies to the walls, leaving free passage for one at a time between the ranks: go out in the cold if you're stupid enough, we'll hang on here a bit! We've been freezing outside all day as it is, why freeze for an extra ten minutes now? We aren't that stupid, you know. You croak today—I'll wait till tomorrow!

Any other time, Shukhov would have propped himself up against the wall with the rest. But now he strode by, sneering.

"What are you afraid of, never seen a Siberian frost before? The wolves are out sunbathing—come and try it! Give a light, old man!"

He lit up just inside the door and went out on the porch. "Wolf's sunshine" was what they jokingly called the moonlight where Shukhov came from.

The moon had risen very high. As far again and it would be at its highest. Sky white with a greenish tinge, stars bright but far between. Snow sparkling white, barracks walls also white. Camp lights might as well not be there.

A crowd of black jackets was growing thicker outside the next hut. They were coming out to line up. And outside that other one. From hut to hut the buzz of conversation was almost drowned out by the crunch of snow under boots.

Five men went down the steps and lined up facing the door. Three others followed them. Shukhov took his place in the second rank with those three. After a munch of bread and with a cig in his mouth, it wasn't too bad standing there. The Latvian hadn't cheated him—it was really good tobacco, heady and sweet-smelling.

Men gradually trickled through the door, and by now there were two or three more ranks of five behind Shukhov. Those already out were in a foul temper. What did the lousy bastards think they were doing, hanging around in the corridor instead of coming outside? Leaving us to freeze.

No zek ever lays eyes on a clock or watch. What good would it do him, anyway? All a zek needs to know is—how soon is reveille? How long till work parade? Till dinnertime? Till lights-out?

Anyway, evening roll call is supposed to be at nine. But that's not the end of it, because they can make you go through the whole rigmarole twice or three times over. You can't get to sleep before ten. And reveille, they figure, is at five. Small wonder that the Moldavian fell asleep just now before quitting time. If a zek manages to get warm, he's asleep right away. By the end of the week there's so much lost sleep to make up for that if you aren't bundled out to work on Sunday the hut is one great heap of sleeping bodies.

Aha—zeks were pouring down from the porch now—the warder and the hut orderly were kicking their behinds. Give it to them, the swine!

"What the hell are you playing at up there?" the front ranks yelled at them. "Skimming the cream from shit? If you'd come out sooner, they'd have finished counting long ago."

The whole hut came tumbling out. Four hundred men—eighty ranks of five. They lined up—neat fives to begin with, then higgledy-piggledy.

"Sort yourselves out at the back there!" the hut orderly roared from the steps.

They don't do it, the bastards.

Tsezar came out hunched up, acting the invalid, followed by two orderlies from the other half of the hut, two from Shukhov's, and another man with a limp. These five became the front rank, so that Shukhov was now in the third. Tsezar was packed off to the rear.

After this, the warder came out onto the porch. "Form up in fives," he shouted at the rear ranks. He had a good pair of tonsils.

"Form up in fives," the hut orderly bellowed. His tonsils were even healthier.

Still they don't move, damn their eyes.

The hut orderly shot down the steps, hurled himself at them, cursing and thumping backs.

He took care which backs he thumped, though. Only the meek were lambasted.

They finally lined up properly. He went back to his place, and shouted with the warder: "First five! Second! Third!"

Each five shot off into the hut as its number was called. Finished for the day.

Unless there's a second roll call, that is. Any herdsman can count better than those good-for-nothings. He may not be able to read, but the whole time he's driving his herd he knows whether all his calves are there or not. This lot are supposed to be trained, but it's done them no good.

The winter before, there'd been no drying rooms in the camp and everybody kept his boots in the barracks overnight—so they'd chased everybody out for a second, a third, or even a fourth count. The men didn't even dress, but rolled out wrapped in their blankets. Since then, drying rooms had been built—not for every hut, but each gang got a chance to dry its boots every third day. So now they'd started doing second counts inside the huts: driving the men from one half to the other.

Shukhov wasn't first in, but he ran without taking his eyes off the one man in front. He hurried to Tsezar's bed, sat on it, and tugged his boots off. Then he climbed up onto a handy bunk and stood his boots on the stove to dry. You just had to get in first. Then back to Tsezar's bed. He sat with his legs tucked under him, one eye watching to see that Tsezar's sack wasn't whipped from under his pillow, the other on the lookout for anybody storming the stove and knocking his boots off their perch.

He had to shout at one man. "Hey! You there, Ginger! Want a boot in your ugly mug? Put your own boots up, but don't touch other people's!"

Zeks were pouring into the hut now. In Gang 20 there were shouts of "Hand over your boots!"

The men taking the boots to the drying room would be let out and the door locked behind them. They'd come running back, shouting: "Citizen warder! Let us in!"

Meanwhile, the warders would gather in the HQ hut with their boards to check their bookkeeping and see whether anyone had escaped.

None of that mattered to Shukhov at present. Ah—here comes Tsezar, diving between the bunks on his way home.

"Thanks, Ivan Denisovich."

Shukhov nodded and scrambled up top like a squirrel. He could finish eating his two hundred grams, he could smoke a second cigarette, or he could just go to sleep.

Only, he was in such high spirits after such a good day he didn't really feel much like sleeping.

Making his bed wasn't much of a job: he just whisked off his blackish blanket, lay down on the mattress (he couldn't have slept on a sheet since he'd left home in '41—in fact, he couldn't for the life of him see why women bothered with sheets, it just made extra washing), laid his head on the pillow stuffed with shavings, shoved his feet into his jerkin, spread his jacket over his blanket, and—

"Thanks be to Thee, O God, another day over!"

He was thankful that he wasn't sleeping in the punishment cell. Here it was just about bearable.

Shukhov lay with his head toward the window, Alyoshka on the other half of the bunk with his head at the other end, where light from the bulb would reach him. He was reading his Testament again.

The lamp wasn't all that far away. They could read or even sew.

Alyoshka heard Shukhov thank God out loud, and looked around.

"There you are, Ivan Denisovich, your soul is asking to be allowed to pray to God. Why not let it have its way, eh?"

Shukhov shot a glance at him: the light in his eyes was like candle flame. Shukhov sighed.

"Because, Alyoshka, prayers are like petitions—either they don't get through at all, or else it's 'complaint rejected.'"

Four sealed boxes stood in front of the staff hut, and were emptied once a month by someone delegated for that purpose. Many prisoners dropped petitions into those boxes, then waited, counting the days, expecting an answer in two months, one month . . .

There would be no answer. Or else—"complaint rejected."

"That's because you never prayed long enough or fervently enough, that's why your prayers weren't answered. Prayer must be persistent. And if you have faith and say to a mountain, 'Make way,' it will make way."

Shukhov grinned, rolled himself another cigarette, and got a light from the Estonian.

"Don't talk rot, Alyoshka. I never saw mountains going anywhere. Come to think of it I've never seen any mountains. But when you and your whole Baptist club did all that praying in the Caucasus, did one single mountain ever move over?"

Poor devils. What harm does their praying do anybody? Collected twenty-five years all around. That's how things are nowadays: twenty-five is the only kind of sentence they hand out.

"We didn't pray for anything like that, Denisych," Alyoshka said earnestly. He moved around with his Testament until he was almost face to face with Shukhov. "The Lord's behest was that we should pray for no earthly or transient thing except our daily bread. 'Give us this day our daily bread.' "

"Our ration, you mean?" Shukhov asked.

Alyoshka went on undeterred, exhorting Shukhov with his eyes more than his words, patting and stroking his hand.

"Ivan Denisovich! We shouldn't pray for somebody to send us a parcel, or for an extra portion of skilly. What people prize highly is vile in the sight of God! We must pray for spiritual things, asking God to remove the scum of evil from our hearts."

"No, you listen to me. There's a priest at our church in Polomnya . . ."

"Don't tell me about your priest!" Alyoshka begged, his brow creased with pain.

"No, you just listen." Shukhov raised himself on his elbow. "In our parish, Polomnya, nobody was better off than the priest. If we got a roofing job, say, we charged other people thirty-five a day but we charged him a hundred. And there was never a peep out of him. He was paying alimony to three women in three different towns and living with his fourth family. The local bishop was under his thumb, our priest greased his palm well. If they sent any other priest along, ours would make his life hell, he wasn't going to share with anybody."

"Why are you telling me about this priest? The Orthodox Church has turned its back on the Gospels—*they* don't get put inside, or else they get off with five years because their faith is not firm."

Shukhov calmly observed Alyoshka's agitation, puffing on his cigarette.

"Look, Alyoshka"—smoke got into the Baptist's eyes as Shukhov pushed his outstretched hand aside—"I'm not against God, see. I'm quite ready to believe in God. But I just don't believe in heaven and hell. Why do you think everybody deserves either heaven or hell? What sort of idiots do you take us for? That's what I don't like."

Shukhov lay back again, after carefully dropping his ash into the space behind his head, between the bunk and the window, so as not to burn the captain's belongings. Lost in thought, he no longer heard Alyoshka's muttering.

"Anyway," he concluded, "pray as much as you like, but they won't knock anything off your sentence. You'll serve your time from bell to bell whatever happens."

Alyoshka was horrified. "That's just the sort of thing you shouldn't pray for! What good is freedom to you? If you're free, your faith will soon be choked by thorns! Be glad you're in prison. Here you have time to think about your soul. Remember what the Apostle Paul says, 'What are you doing, weeping and breaking my heart? For I am ready not only to be imprisoned but even to die in Jerusalem for the name of the Lord Jesus.' "[23]

Shukhov stared at the ceiling and said nothing. He no longer knew whether he wanted to be free or not. To begin with, he'd wanted it very much, and counted up every evening how many days he still had to serve. Then he'd got fed up with it. And still later it had gradually dawned on him that people like himself were not allowed to go home but were packed off into exile. And there was no knowing where the living was easier—here or there.

The one thing he might want to ask God for was to let him go home. But *they* wouldn't let him go home.

Alyoshka wasn't lying, though. You could tell from his voice and his eyes that he was glad to be in prison.

"Look, Alyoshka," Shukhov explained, "it's worked out pretty well for you. Christ told you to go to jail, and you did it, for Christ. But what am I here for? Because they weren't ready for the war in '41—is that the reason? Was that my fault?"

"No second roll call, by the look of it," Kildigs growled from his bed. He yawned.

"Wonders never cease," Shukhov said. "Maybe we can get some sleep."

At that very minute, just as the hut was growing quiet, they heard the rattle of a bolt at the outer door of the hut. The two men who'd taken the boots to be dried dashed into the hut shouting, "Second roll call!"

A warder followed them, shouting, "Out into the other half!"

Some of them were already sleeping! They all began stirring, grumbling and groaning as they drew their boots on (very few of them were in their

---

23. Acts 21:13.

underpants—they mostly slept as they were, in their padded trousers—without them, your feet would be frozen stiff even under a blanket).

Shukhov swore loudly. "Damn them to hell!" But he wasn't all that angry, because he hadn't fallen asleep yet.

Tsezar's hand reached up to place two biscuits, two lumps of sugar, and one round chunk of sausage on Shukhov's bed.

"Thank you, Tsezar Markovich," Shukhov said, lowering his head into the gangway between bunks. "Better give me your bag to put under my pillow for safety." (A passing zek's thieving hands wouldn't find it so quickly up there—and anyway, who would expect Shukhov to have anything?)

Tsezar passed his tightly tied white bag up to Shukhov. Shukhov tucked it under his mattress and was going to wait a bit until more men had been herded out so that he wouldn't have to stand barefoot on the corridor floor so long. But the warder snarled at him: "You over there! In the corner!"

So Shukhov sprang to the floor, landing lightly on his bare feet (his boots and foot rags were so cozy up there on the stove it would be a pity to move them). He had cobbled so many pairs of slippers—but always for others, never for himself. Still, he was used to it, and it wouldn't be for long.

Slippers were confiscated if found in the daytime.

The gangs who'd handed in their boots for drying were all right now if they had slippers, but some had only foot rags tied around their feet, and others were barefoot.

"Get on with it! Get on with it!" the warder roared.

The hut orderly joined in: "Want a bit of the stick, you scum?"

Most of them were crammed into the other half of the hut, with the last few crowding into the corridor. Shukhov stood against the partition wall by the night bucket. The floor was damp to his feet, and an icy draft blew along it from the lobby.

Everybody was out now, but the warder and the hut orderly went to look yet again to see whether anybody was hiding, or curled up asleep in a dark spot. Too few or too many at the count meant trouble—yet another recheck. The two of them went around and around, then came back to the door.

One by one, but quickly now, they were allowed back in. Shukhov squeezed in eighteenth, dashed to his bunk, hoisted his foot onto a bracket, and—heave-ho!—up he went.

Great. Feet into his jerkin sleeve again, blanket on top, jacket over that, and we're asleep! All the zeks in the other half of the barracks would now be herded into our half—but that was their bad luck.

Tsezar came back. Shukhov lowered the bag to him.

Now Alyoshka was back. He had no sense at all, Alyoshka, never earned a thing, but did favors for everybody.

"Here you are, Alyoshka!" Shukhov handed him one biscuit.

Alyoshka was all smiles. "Thank you! You won't have any for yourself!"

"Eat it!"

If we're without, we can always earn something.

He himself took the lump of sausage—and popped it into his mouth. Get the teeth to it. Chew, chew, chew! Lovely meaty smell! Meat juice, the real thing. Down it went, into his belly.

End of sausage.

The other stuff he planned to eat before work parade.

He covered his head with the skimpy, grubby blanket and stopped listening to the zeks from the other half crowding in between the bunks to be counted.

Shukhov felt pleased with life as he went to sleep. A lot of good things had happened that day. He hadn't been thrown in the hole. The gang hadn't been dragged off to Sotsgorodok. He'd swiped the extra gruel at dinnertime. The foreman had got a good rate for the job. He'd enjoyed working on the wall. He hadn't been caught with the blade at the search point. He'd earned a bit from Tsezar that evening. And he'd bought his tobacco.

The end of an unclouded day. Almost a happy one.

Just one of the 3,653 days of his sentence, from bell to bell.

The extra three were for leap years.

1959

Related Readings

Irina Eremia
Bragin

Teach Your Children

*Irina Eremia Bragin's father endured years as a political
prisoner in Romania and then was not allowed to leave the
country. As a result, his daughter was separated from him
for twenty-five years while she grew up and started her
own family in the United States. In this article, she finds
a message for herself and her children in her father's
determination to survive without losing his ideals.*

WHO IS YOUR HERO and why do you admire him?" is the question my
11-year-old son must answer on his application to private secondary school.
At the open house for this much-sought-after school, the headmaster made
a speech linking the growing incidence of drug abuse, suicide and violence
among teenagers to the absence of heroes in contemporary life. He suggested
that the two California girls who shot themselves, leaving behind treasure-
hunt maps leading their classmates to their bodies, sacrificed their lives for
the sake of notoriety, perhaps mistaking it for a kind of immortality. Why
should we be shocked by such self-destructive acts, he asked, when our media
reward outrageous behavior—the more outrageous the better—with instant
celebrity? Growing up without paradigms[1] of heroic action, in a society where
the merely sensational increasingly wins the spotlight, many adolescents
seek to distinguish themselves through desperate, violent acts.

I couldn't have agreed with him more. But I also wondered whether this
eloquent[2] speaker had ever known a real hero or considered the price that
might be paid for a genuine act of courage. As the daughter of a prisoner of
conscience, I cannot speak lightly to my children about heroes. From the

---

1. **paradigms** examples
2. **eloquent** forceful, fluent

moment I found myself face to face with my father after our 25-year separation, I have been exploring my feelings toward the man whose act of courage resulted in my growing up fatherless.

The man in the black suit and wide-brimmed hat now walking hesitantly up the ramp from customs looks Romanian. Is he my father? Should I run up and hug him? I press through the throng gathered to meet the Pan Am flight from Bucharest.

"*Bine ai venit!*" I hear a voice behind me, and another woman runs up and kisses the man in the black suit on both cheeks. My mistake terrifies me. What if I don't recognize him? Twenty-five years ago, when I said goodbye to him at the airport in Bucharest for what we thought might be forever, I was not yet 12 years old, a frightened little girl on her way to an unknown land. Even then, I had had only eight months since his release from prison to get reacquainted with him before he signed the form giving his ex-wife permission to take his children out of the country. My father encouraged us to go, knowing he might never see us again.

Suddenly I spot him. There's no doubt in my mind. The round, warm face, the blue eyes now sparkling with tears—my blue eyes, my children's blue eyes. We exchange the traditional Romanian greetings:

"*Bine ai venit!*" (It's good to see you!)

"*Bine te-am gasit!*" (It's good to be here!)

His familiar voice pushes memory back, beyond the bewildered 11-year-old girl shrinking fearfully from the emaciated[3] man with missing teeth who had suddenly materialized, coming again into her childhood as inexplicably as six years before he had vanished from it. His voice awakens memories of a time before his disappearance and all the questions, rumors, doubts; a time when a little girl competed with her big brother for a larger share of their father's chest, where they rested their heads as he crooned "*Somnoroase Pasarele*" (My Sleepy Little Birds). Now a parent myself, I, too, have sung "*Somnoroase Pasarele*" to my sleepy little birds as I kissed them and rocked them to sleep.

I embrace him, trying not to cry. There are no flashing camera lights or TV reporters waiting to greet Ion Eremia, only two children who have grown up without him and two grandchildren whom he has never met.

My father's visit took place in the spring of 1990, several months after the "spontaneous revolution" that overthrew Nicolae Ceausescu. The events in Romania were the climax of that absorbing drama—The Fall of the House of Communism—that unfolded so rapidly before our astonished

---

3. **emaciated** very thin

eyes at the end of the 1980s. It was a romantic play that filled spectators with faith and optimism. Glasnost had triumphed in Russia. The Berlin Wall was gone. A dissident playwright in Czechoslovakia and a rebel union chief in Poland became the triumphant leaders of their long-suffering nations. Capitalism proved stronger than communism. Francis Fukuyama declared that we had reached "the end of history."

As the Iron Curtain rose, the spotlight fell on Romania, which offered the most dramatic spectacle of all: A once-wealthy nation brought to utter ruin. Hungry, frightened citizens, moving like shadows on dark, frozen streets, scavenging for food. Neglected orphans rocking themselves for comfort, staring into space with desperate eyes. A pair of wicked tyrants terrorizing their subjects from their magnificent palace filled with stolen treasures. Suddenly, at a routine rally, instead of the rehearsed cheers, the despot is booed and hooted from his balcony. Heroic young men and women, willing to throw themselves in front of tanks and bullets, lead the oppressed masses to revolt. The vicious tyrant and his vile consort try to flee through the labyrinthine[4] tunnels beneath their palace. After a fierce chase, they are captured, tried and finally executed. Their grotesque bodies lie side by side in a pool of blood in the muddy snow. The liberated slaves dance in the streets of their ravaged cities.

For many Americans, this fairy-tale-like sequence of events put Romania on the map. The media were as obsessed then with Nicolae and Elena Ceausescu (Macbeth and Lady Macbeth) as they were recently with O. J. and Nicole Simpson (Othello and Desdemona)—though not for as long.

For me, the events in Romania had deep personal implications. My father and Ceausescu had once been colleagues, having been appointed co-vice ministers of defense in 1952, a year before my birth. My father and Ceausescu were also political and personal enemies.

Ion Eremia was a career officer in the Romanian army who had joined the Communist underground—the only organized opposition to the government's collaboration with the Nazis—during World War II. When he fell in love with my mother, Regina Boian, a beautiful and talented young actress whom he first saw on stage, he was a general, one of the few well-educated Communists in the army and a rising star in the new regime. But unlike his colleague Ceausescu, Ion was an idealist, and quickly awakened to the corruption of his dreams. Unable to repress his outrage, he was dismissed from his post for criticizing the system. Undaunted, he proceeded to write a satirical political allegory, *Gulliver in the Land of Lies*, which exposed the hypocrisy of communism-in-practice. He entrusted the manuscript to an old childhood friend, a sailor, who was to smuggle it out of the

---

4. **labyrinthine** complex; mazelike

country to a French publisher. The friend turned out to be an informer. In 1958, my father was arrested, tried in secret and condemned to 25 years in prison for "the intent to publish" a book that "spread lies about the government." My mother might have gone to prison, too, had my parents not divorced only weeks before his arrest, in anticipation of that possibility. Instead, she lost her home and her job, and was never allowed to appear on stage again.

For the next six years my father's whereabouts were unknown. I was told that "Neclo," as my brother and I called our father, had gone abroad on business, an explanation I believed despite the whispers, the insults from other children, the persecution from teachers and our dramatic change in lifestyle. By 1964, when all political prisoners had been granted amnesty as part of an overture by Romania toward the West, I had stopped asking questions about "Neclo."

I didn't see my father until two days after his return, and then quite by accident. When he couldn't find us at our old address, he went to his sister's house, and it was there that my mother went to meet him. Shocked by his emaciated appearance and worried that we'd be frightened, she asked him to take some time to recuperate before seeing his children. But fate willed otherwise. Instead of walking home after school as usual, my girlfriend and I decided to stop at the Lupoaica, a quaint little park in Bucharest built around an ancient statue of Romulus and Remus. Facing the statue was a bench, and there my friend and I sat next to a thin, bald man with missing teeth. Suddenly, I noticed him staring at me.

"What's your name?" he asked me.

"Irina Eremia."

He searched through his pockets and pulled out a small bread roll wrapped in a paper napkin.

"Take this. It's fresh!" he said.

I grabbed my girlfriend's hand and ran away. I wouldn't tell her why.

An hour later, the emaciated stranger knocked at my door. I could see him through the keyhole. I was alone in the house. Still, I let him in.

"Don't you know who I am? It's me, Neclo!"

I noticed that his deep-set blue eyes were watering. He reached out to hug me with two long, thin, bony arms. I turned away.

During the next eight months, we almost overcame the barriers erected by the six lost years. But just as we were becoming a family again, the Romanian leader, Gheorghe Gheorghiu-Dej, who had been liberalizing the country's policies, was suddenly reported dead and Nicolae Ceausescu was named his successor. My parents foresaw disaster. "Me, they'll never let out, but perhaps you and the children can go," my father told my mother. She was Jewish; he was not. We could take advantage of the newly expanded

Jewish emigration quotas. My mother, brother and I applied to join the rest of my mother's family in California. My father signed a form giving his consent. For the next 25 years, while Ceausescu was in power, we could only keep in touch by letter.

Several days before my father was due to arrive in the United States for our reunion, I watched a network interview with a Romanian journalist who had collaborated with Ceausescu's regime. Asked why she had consented to violate the standards of her profession, the Romanian answered, "I had to survive. All of us did what we could to survive." The American correspondent wouldn't let her get off so easily. Politely, she suggested that some people prefer to die with honor rather than betray their principles. "Don't you think you owe your people an apology?" she asked, as the Romanian journalist hung her head in shame. Watching this, I remembered an old Romanian saying: "It is easy to suffer 24 lashes on someone else's behind."

As my father's daughter, I fully understood the moral complexity of the choices he made. For more than a quarter of a century, until history turned the tables in Romania, most of my father's acquaintances as well as his own relatives (some of whom were demoted from their jobs in reprisal for his acts) considered him not a hero, but a failure, who had destroyed his brilliant career, ruined his marriage and broken up his family. What had he gained, they asked, by stubbornly adhering to his principles? Just look at his former colleague, Ceausescu, not nearly as bright, or capable, or handsome, or charismatic, who had risen to lead the country and elevate every member of his family to a position of power!

Would the slick, self-confident American correspondent who was now standing in judgment of her Romanian counterpart have risked her own family and her own career, or even less important things—her membership in her country club, her position on the board of her children's school, her reputation in her neighborhood—for the sake of her principles, I wondered. How many people are willing to risk anything of real value to themselves for the sake of a principle, an ideal, a standard? Why should they, anyway?

I have struggled with this question most of my life. For if I am the daughter of a man who would not abandon his principles for any price, I am also the daughter of a woman who had to suffer the consequences of her husband's acts of conscience, bravely pick up the pieces of her family's shattered life, stubbornly teach her children how to survive and strive and hold their heads up in a hostile environment, lick their wounds, put bread on their table and then start a new life from scratch in a foreign country, alone, with two children.

In my years of growing up, I saw my mother as a larger-than-life figure, a heroine who always triumphed over the obstacles thrown in our way.

Strong, determined, a fighter, she refused to allow herself to be defeated by hardships. She raised my brother and me to believe in ourselves and our future—even when she was told that for us there would be no future. . . .

My father helps my son build a tall tower out of sand. Farther from the surf, I lie on a chaise lounge and read selections from my father's prison memoir, which he wrote in his mind while in prison and preserved in his memory until shortly before his visit, when he finally put it on paper. He brought me a few chapters, still too uncertain about the new regime to risk taking the entire manuscript through customs.

This is my first chance to hear my father's side of the story, his version of the events that changed our lives:

> *I had every reason to be happy with my life: a lovely wife, two beautiful children, a successful career. But every day I drove in my limousine past long lines of desperate, starving people, endlessly waiting at stores whose shelves were bare. My wife begged me to keep my mouth shut and think about my family. Did I want my children to grow up orphans? So many were arrested, so many disappeared. Why flirt with self-destruction? What could I possibly hope to accomplish, anyway?*
>
> *I could have chosen to look away, to bury my nose in the very important papers on my desk. But how could I?*

I was 5 in September 1958, when my father was arrested. Before the night of his disappearance, we had lived a charmed life. Our old, stately house and its large, beautiful garden, with its pear, apple, apricot and quince trees, remains the Paradise Lost of my memories. I remember red rose bushes and white butterflies. I remember a hen, Albuta, who used to lay a fresh egg for my breakfast every morning. And I remember running to the gate to meet a tall man wearing a white jacket with epaulets,[5] medals and shiny gold buttons who would lift me up, up, up and kiss my cheeks. His mustache tickled me and made me giggle. Then one morning he was not there at breakfast to walk me to kindergarten and kiss me goodbye. My mother said that he would be back soon, very soon. I believed her even when we had to leave everything and hastily move in with my grandmother, and even later when children pelted me with snowballs and called me "convict's daughter," and still later when my best friend told me that her parents wouldn't allow her to play with me anymore because my father was a criminal. "You're a liar!" I shouted at the closing door.

Whether committed as a result of faith or foolishness, my father's acts of

---

5. **epaulets** ornamental shoulder pads on military uniforms

conscience cost him dearly. Stretched out on the beach with his manuscript, I see him alone, in his cold, dark cell, counting the footsteps of the guard who comes to peer at him through a slit in the door every five minutes. As the steps recede, nimbly, like a cat, he jumps up on his stool and stares through the bars of his tiny window at his "enchanted isle"—the tops of seven poplar trees and, through them, a patch of sky. The guard's footsteps approach again. My father jumps back down and resumes position, head bent, hands crossed over his belly. He is not allowed to talk to anyone or to do anything. To pass the time, he listens to an imaginary symphony, experiencing the music as intensely as if it were real. A factory siren wails. Protected by its shriek, he begins to sing a popular Romanian ballad about his beloved Carpathian Mountains, their high cliffs, lush meadows, dense forests, clear streams . . . When he is finally taken from his cell for his solitary 15-minute walk in the prison courtyard, he must keep his eyes on the ground; under no circumstances may he look up at the sky. "I thirst for the sky," he cries in one of the poems he composed in prison:

From my dark cave,
From my deep grave,
Under bolts of ice,
Under waves of fog,
I miss endlessly
That blue infinity.
How I thirst . . . thirst for the sky.

"A beautiful dream!" my father exclaims again and again throughout our vacation at the shore. As tireless as my children, this determined 76-year-old man doesn't want to miss anything. He's in excellent physical shape. His proud bearing and powerful build make him look taller than his height and younger than his years. "Americans are happy people," he declares, watching the families picnicking on the beach. His eyes are wistful, the dreamy eyes of a writer. They laugh and sparkle, and his face lights up in childish merriment as he jumps the waves, chases my children, learns to throw a Frisbee, eats hamburgers and french fries. So many things we take for granted—the little packages of sugar, cream, mustard and ketchup available to everyone at the food stands, the groaning shelves at the supermarket, the well-lit freeways, the magical efficiency of the McDonald's drive-through—delight and amaze him. But as he is entering our bright, abundant world, I am plunging into the world of his past. As we view the sights, take a harbor tour and pose for pictures, my father's verses resonate in my mind:

Come, children, again,
Stealthily, tonight,
Late, when jailers sleep,
Late, when hunger wakes,
My infinite yearning,
Dissolving these walls of stone.

My father and the children are splashing in the motel pool; I sit on the side, reading the chapter "The Coughed Prayer":

> *It was the third day of Christmas, St. Stefan's day. Lost in memories, I didn't at first notice the loud coughs in the cell on my right. It was my neighbor, the Catholic priest, the only prisoner among us granted the right to cough out loud—he suffered from tuberculosis. I realized that his coughs followed the Morse code signals we used to communicate with each other through knocks on the wall. I deciphered a short cough, a dot, followed by a double cough, a dash. The priest was using his special privilege to convey a prayer to St. Stefan, on behalf of the condemned. He repeated his prayer twice and I finally understood it: "Saint Stefan, you, the first martyr of Christianity, listen to our fervent prayer, destroy our chains and deliver us from our torturers. Amen." When I was brought out for my solitary walk in the courtyard, I noticed that the new snow was stained with a circle of blood. For the next few nights I desperately tapped message after message to the priest. No one answered. My neighbor remained silent. He had paid for his prayer with his life.*

A small wet hand touches my cheek. "Why are you crying, Mommy?" asks my 3-year-old girl.

"The sun's in my eye, darling." I wrap her in a towel, hold her shivering body next to mine, and wonder: Was it worth it? My father was robbed of our childhood. Was it worth losing his children for the sake of his ideals? . . .

As I work on translating the prison chronicle, I realize it was my father's rich imagination, which in his youth drew him to the promise of a socialist paradise, that enabled him later, in conditions of extremity, to transform physical suffering into spiritual triumph. Like my mother, my father is a survivor, but of a different kind. The practical wisdom of people like my mother enables us to live; the romantic vision of people like my father gives us something to live for.

Dragging himself home, barefoot and in rags, to the family he hopes is still waiting, the newly released prisoner is filled not with bitterness for his wrongful suffering but with gratitude for his spiritual growth.

I'm awake! I'm alive! I confessed nothing! I signed nothing! My spirit is intact! My will is even stronger and my mind more agile than when I first entered the realm of cold, hunger, loneliness and immobility. I learned to sing without sound and to write without paper. Despite everything, man remains the most marvelous, the most accomplished creature wrought by nature! For this reason we must never lose faith in his greatness, in his right to be valued and, yes, to be loved.

This, I promise myself, is what I'll tell my children, as I encourage them to nourish their souls, strengthen their characters and give shape to their dreams.

"I finished the application essay!" my son announces, bursting into my room. He has been working hard on it for many hours. I read it, tears streaming down my cheeks:

> *Last summer I got to know a real hero. My mom, dad, sister and I went to France. My mom's father, Neclo, who lives in Bucharest, Romania, came there to meet us. Neclo is a hero.*
>
> *When my mother was a little girl, her father was put in prison for speaking out against the government. After six years of being shut up alone, in a dungeon, he was released. Then my mother, uncle and grandmother left the country. Neclo was not allowed to leave with them.*
>
> *I had met my grandfather one time before, when I was six years old and he came to America to visit us. It was the first time he was allowed to see his family in twenty-five years, because there was finally a revolution in Romania against the tyrant that kept everyone a slave. But my grandfather only stayed with us for a few months. He didn't speak much English. He felt he was too old to start a new life. I was sad when he went back to Romania but I kind of understood how he felt.*
>
> *In France we stayed in a small town called Andlau. It was quiet and beautiful. There were acres and acres of vineyards, one right behind the small inn where we stayed. It was a relaxing, peaceful place, and Neclo and I had a chance to play ball, cards and chess and just be together. He had studied English and he could speak better than before. Mostly, we communicated with our eyes and gestures. I tried to let him know that I cared for him, even though he is not part of my life, like Grandpa, my dad's dad.*
>
> *We also took day trips and visited some of the castles in the area. We saw the dungeons where the prisoners were kept. Some still had the prisoners' names carved in the walls. I understood how brave Neclo had to be to stand being locked away in a cell by himself.*
>
> *Learning about Neclo has made standing up for my beliefs very*

important to me. In fifth grade I wrote my teacher a letter of protest when I felt she had made an unfair decision regarding one of my friends. I am now the student council representative for my class and am fighting hard to make things better at our school. I'm proud of my Romanian grandfather. I hope I get to see him again!

"I'll send a copy to Neclo," I tell him, hoping that my son's gift will make up for all the gifts he and his grandfather have never shared.

**Margaret
Shapiro**

The First Gulag Returns to Its Monastic Roots

During Joseph Stalin's regime, a system of forced labor prisons provided the workers for government projects. Political dissidents, members of minority groups, writers and artists, and common criminals were caught in the system, called the Gulag. Stalin took his model for the prisons from an isolated monastery on an island near the Arctic Circle, where earlier rulers of Russia had exiled their political enemies. By 1936 nearly five million people were imprisoned in the Gulag system.

SOLOVETSKY ISLAND, RUSSIA—In the huge expanse of Russia, few places seem as remote as this windblown northern island in the White Sea, where the Gulf Stream ends and children wear wool hats all year round.

Yet for centuries people have come here: Medieval monks, who sought isolation and eventually built a walled, fairy-tale monastery; Bolshevik commissars, who made the island a prototype[1] for all the brutal prison camps still to come; the Soviet navy, which manned a vigilant outpost against the West; and now businessmen, who have filled the island's small grocery with jars of spaghetti sauce and Snickers bars.

Uniting them all have been the unimaginable difficulty of life near the Arctic Circle and a seemingly irrational determination to live here nonetheless. This is an island, after all, with two seasons: winter (11 months) and mosquito (30 varieties). In the few weeks of relative warmth, when the thermometer climbs into the low 50s, the hardy residents of Solovetsky Island ceaselessly chop firewood for the coming winter. In December and January, the sun never rises; in July, it never sets.

"For many people this is a very hard life," acknowledged Mikhail

---

1. **prototype** original model

Verwald, a shaggy-haired guide for the local historical museum, who left Moscow four years ago for the peace and isolation of Solovki, as the island is known. "I like it here."

The village that has sprouted here is a threadbare specimen, above which towers the still impressive though crumbling monastery. Most of Solovki's 1,300 residents live in wooden houses or converted prison-camp barracks. The few streets in its center are not paved, and the ones in the outskirts are so dusty and rock-strewn that a ride over them on the island's rickety bus is a bone-jolting affair. A few teenagers careen[2] around on motorbikes. Everywhere cows and muddy sheep graze among purple and pink wildflowers, avoiding the elevated wooden planks that function as sidewalks during so many months of snow or oozing mud.

People have been living here since the 15th century, when two solitude-seeking monks sailed across the frigid White Sea and found exactly what they sought. Over the next few hundred years, the grand Russian Orthodox monastery grew, surrounded by huge white walls and towers built out of the immense boulders left strewn around the island by retreating Arctic glaciers.

Soon it also became a place of political exile for those who displeased the czars. From Ivan the Terrible on, noblemen and others who fell out of favor or engaged in plots ended up here to live out their lives as monks. It was a perfect prison, remote and surrounded by a sea that in winter doesn't freeze enough to walk on and in summer is too cold to swim in and survive.

But it was under the Soviet regime that this island and the five smaller ones around it became a lasting symbol of a more barbaric sort. Here the Bolsheviks developed an early prototype—before Hitler and his concentration camps—of what the world now knows as the Stalinist gulag, where millions of Russians eventually perished at the hands of their own rulers and countrymen.

"It was the camp on which all future norms were designed: how much food to give, what kind of clothing, how to execute people and get rid of their bodies," said Yuri Brodsky, a historian of the islands. "It was a micro-model of the whole horrible system."

In 1923, the new Soviet government ordered the monastery closed and the monks sent away. In their place in the churches and prayer cells came the first "class enemies": aristocrats, chemists, linguists, military men, lawyers, historians, artists. At first, the regimen was not that bad. It was cold and the prisoners were poorly clothed and fed, and many were shot, but others were allowed to walk freely inside the monastery and even establish a theater, a newspaper and study groups.

But by the late 1920s the regime in Moscow had hardened, and so too

---

2. **careen** rush carelessly

had life on Solovki. A children's colony, for "counterrevolutionaries" age 12 to 16, was set up. Thousands of prisoners arrived each day in summer and were stuffed into dank, airless chambers already crammed full. Tortures, such as standing a prisoner naked for hours in a swarm of mosquitoes or pouring cold water over him and letting him freeze in the snow, were finely honed to break people physically and psychologically. Mass executions occurred regularly, with dozens at a time dragged out on blustery winter nights, hand-cuffed and dressed only in underwear, to be shot and dumped in huge pits.

"They were shot in the back of their heads," recalled philosopher and historian Dimitry Likhachev, who was imprisoned here for four years. "The executioner and others were drunk, so they did not always manage to shoot people to death right away, but they threw them in the pit all the same. The pit, covered with soil, showed signs of movement even on the day after the shooting."

No one knows how many died—maybe 10,000 of the 60,000 to 80,000 who were imprisoned here, many not inside the monastery but at remote, primitive logging camps scattered among the islands.

In 1939 the labor camp was disbanded and its surviving prisoners sent to suffer elsewhere. Soviet dictator Joseph Stalin had decided that Solovki was too close to Finland and, in a war, the enemy might discover the Soviet Union's concentration camps.

The island was turned into a military training school for the Northern Fleet, which was based nearby in Murmansk. The monastery was converted into housing, schools and clinics for the soldiers; its remaining frescoes and icons were used for target practice or as building materials. In 1962 the military moved out and the islands were turned into a historic and nature preserve. Locals began to visit again and settle here. A few years later the museum opened, but it was forbidden to mention anything that had hap-pened after 1923.

"That was hidden history," said Alexander Martynov, head of the museum, who has lived on Solovki for nearly two decades. When local con-struction workers inadvertently dug into one of the mass graves, turning up bones and scraps of clothing, KGB officials quickly arrived to cover it up and instructed everyone to forget what they saw, Martynov said.

After Mikhail Gorbachev came to power in 1985, his policy of openness allowed the full story of Solovki to begin to come out. The huge red Soviet star, similar to those festooning[3] the Kremlin in Moscow, was taken down in 1986. The collapse of communism [in 1991] completed the process. The museum, operating inside the monastery walls, now has a stark display about the victims and the system of repression that was honed so successfully here.

---

3. **festooning** decorating

Among the artifacts is a final desperate missive written by a man who suspected he would never see the mainland again. "My family lives in Pskov," he wrote, "my wife, my daughter and my son. I kiss them all. S. Fedotov." The letter, and thousands others like it, were found undelivered in rubbish heaps.

Today, a few people can remember those years but would rather not.

"I lived through it," recalled Natalia Sysoyeva, 77, whose husband, an illiterate farm boy, was sent here from southern Russia to be a prison guard and who herself worked inside the monastery walls as a cleaner. "It was all 'hurry up and don't talk.' There wasn't any time to think about it. It was a military secret. We just did what we were told."

Mostly, like the rest of Russia, Solovki is moving on. The monastery was reconsecrated several years ago and is being restored. Fifteen monks and a similar number of initiates[4] now live in it. Russian and foreign tourists come here daily throughout the summer to visit a place known for its harsh climate and harsh history.

Like everywhere else, people here grouse[5] about the high prices of Russia's post-Soviet free market. But they also marvel at how much is available in the little local stores. There are even local businessmen, about 20 of them, who bring in imported food, color television sets and Chinese-made down parkas.

Martynov, the museum director, said he feels generally optimistic about the future. But Russian history, as viewed from Solovki, gives reason for pause, he acknowledged.

"It would be nice to think that this kind of thing couldn't happen again," he said. "But during a crisis time, it's hard to be 100 percent sure. The Russian people are capable of doing anything, good or bad. One generation builds, the next destroys. The third rebuilds. And what the fourth will do, no one knows."

---

4. **initiate** someone properly admitted to membership or an office
5. **grouse** complain

retold by
Charles Downing

Death and the Soldier

This folktale reveals that an old soldier's life was never easy in Russia. The early rulers as well as later oppressive regimes felt little obligation to their common soldiers. Like the former soldiers in Ivan Denisovich's labor camp, the soldier of this story can expect no reward for his service to his country.

A LONG TIME AGO in Russia there lived a Soldier who served the Tsar faithfully for the space of twenty-five years, fighting his battles on many fronts and receiving, alas! far more grievous wounds than golden coins. At the end of his twenty-fifth year in the Army, when he had grown old and was no good to fight any more, he was summoned by his captain.

"Soldier," said the officer, "you have served the Tsar faithfully for many years and have always performed your service well. But now that you are old the Army can no longer afford to keep you. You are therefore released from military service and may now go home. Private Ivan, dismiss!"

The Soldier saluted, turned about, slung his knapsack over his shoulder, and marched away smartly. But though his step was as brisk as ever, his heart was heavy with sadness.

"For twenty-five long years I have served the Tsar," he thought, "and now that I am no longer considered to be of any use to him, I am sent away with only three dry biscuits to stand between me and starvation. What can a poor old soldier do, and where shall he lay his head? There is nothing for it but to return to my native village, back to my old father and mother, and if they are no longer of the world of the living, I shall just lie down beside them in the grave and die."

On and on he marched, and one day passed and then another until all that remained in his old battered knapsack was one lone biscuit. This he saved as long as his stomach could endure it, for his home was many miles away. When hunger rattled hollowly within him, however, and he could stand it no more, he sat down under a tree, took out the one dry biscuit, and was about to eat it when his eyes fell on a ragged old beggar standing before him.

"I am hungry, Soldier," said the beggar. "Give me charity, for the love of God."

"Ah, well," sighed the Soldier. "I am an old sweat and still have a trick or two up my sleeve. Something is bound to turn up. But where should this poor old beggar turn if he is hungry?"

He handed the biscuit to the old man, lit his pipe, straightened his crumpled tunic, and set out once again along the road for home, marching on and on along the hard, dusty road with the hot sun burning down on him.

Suddenly he stopped dead in his tracks. A flock of wild geese were swimming on the surface of a lake.

"Here's a stroke of luck!" muttered the Soldier, and ducking swiftly among the bushes, he unslung his rifle, took careful aim, and with three quick and skilful shots knocked off as many geese.

"I shall not starve to death yet awhile," he murmured as he picked the geese up and stuffed them in his empty rucksack, and striding gaily on into town, he came to a halt before an old ramshackle farm-house. He knocked loudly on the door, and when it opened and an aged peasant appeared in the doorway, he thrust the three geese into his hands.

"Take these three geese, batiushka."[1] he said. "Roast one for me, keep the second for yourself as payment for your trouble, and in exchange for the third give me a goodly measure of wine to wash down my roast goose!"

That evening in the old farm-house the Soldier ate a meal fit for the Tsar, and the borsch,[2] the roast goose, and the strong wine made his belly roll with a contentment it had not known for many a day. As he pushed his plate away with a happy sigh and lit his old pipe, his eye chanced to fall on a palatial mansion situated on the opposite side of the road.

"That's a fine building, batiushka," he said idly. "To whom does it belong?"

"That," replied his host, filling two cups of tea from the boiling samovar,[3] "was built by the richest merchant in town."

"He's a lucky fellow to have such a place to live in."

"He *would* be," replied the peasant, "if only he could *live* there. But he dare not move in."

---

1. **batiushka** old man
2. **borsch** also, *borscht;* beet soup
3. **samovar** urn with a spigot, used to boil water for tea

"Dare not move in?" repeated the Soldier incredulously. "Why not?"

"Unclean spirits have seized the whole house. Every night a host of demons gather in it and shriek and shout and dance about until the light of dawn. All night long the place is in an uproar and the folk who live in these parts are too terrified to go near the place after dusk."

"That is interesting," said the Soldier. "Where might I find the owner of this house, for I should like to ask him whether there is anything I could do to help?"

The peasant stared at the Soldier as if he had gone mad, but reflecting that twenty-five years in the Army would soften the brain of any man, he told him what he wanted to know. The Soldier lay down on the stove to rest after his fine dinner, and when evening came, he rose, went into town, and sought out the rich merchant.

"What can I do for you, Soldier?" the merchant asked, somewhat absently, for he was a worried man.

"I am on my way home," replied the Soldier, "and have nowhere to spend the night. I should be very grateful if you would allow me to sleep in your big new house down the road, for I have observed that it is quite empty."

"Are you mad?" exclaimed the merchant. "It would be suicide! Sleep anywhere else—for there are houses enough in this town—but for Heaven's sake do not think of entering that accursed new house of mine! As soon as I had the roof on, half the demons of Hell moved in. There is no getting rid of them."

"Let's not look on the dark side of things," said the Soldier. "You never know, the demons might jump to it at the command of an old sweat like me."

"Don't think you are the first to try to rid the house of this devil's brood, Soldier," said the merchant. "Others have undertaken the task, and all have failed. Last summer a fellow volunteered to drive them out of the house and had the courage to spend the night in it. All that remained of *him* the next morning was a heap of bones sucked white and dry!"

"We have a saying in the Army, merchant: 'Water will not drown the Russian soldier nor fire burn him.' I've served with the colours for most of my life, and many's the narrow escape I've had in countless battles and campaigns. But I've always come out alive and kicking and I should not like anyone to think that I should retreat or surrender in the face of a mere devil or so."

"Have it your own way," replied the merchant. "If you are not afraid I shall not try to deter you. Indeed, if you do manage to drive these evil spirits from my house, I shall not be sparing with your reward."

"All right," said the Soldier. "Now if you could get me a few candles, some dried nuts, and one large boiled beetroot . . ."

"Come into the store and take whatever you need," said the merchant, and following him into the shop, the Soldier helped himself to a dozen candles, three pounds of dried nuts and one large boiled beetroot, and with this strange equipment he marched confidently off to the new mansion just as night was beginning to fall. He entered the house, made himself comfortable in the bedroom, hung his greatcoat and knapsack on a hook, and lit the candles. Then he puffed away at his pipe, and cracking the dry nuts in his fingers, waited calmly and patiently for something to happen.

On the stroke of midnight a loud shriek of fiendish laughter echoed through the empty house, and this, it appeared, was the signal for a veritable[4] bedlam[5] to break loose, for on all sides and in every corner of the house doors slammed, walls rattled, ceilings shook, cloven hooves danced and clumped on the floorboards and blood-curdling screams rang through the air. The Soldier was puffing away at his pipe as though nothing had happened, when suddenly the door of the bedroom was pushed open, a red, horned head poked round the door, and the glowing green eyes of a devil lit up with demoniac glee.

"I've found a man! I've found a man!" he shrieked. "Oh, what a feast we'll have now!"

There was a squeal of joy and a scurry of a thousand furry feet, and in a trice a host of devils crowded in the doorway, hustling and bustling and elbowing each other in their enthusiasm.

"Tear him to pieces and eat him up!" they shrieked.

"Just come and try it!" said the Soldier, with a threatening glare. "I've never seen such a lousy crew in all my life! I've killed better devils than you a dozen at a time, so shut up, or else . . ."

In the face of this somewhat unexpected reception, the multitude of devils shrank back in some alarm. The largest of them was likewise daunted by the menacing tone of the Soldier, but urged on by his companions, he stepped forward with a show of bravado.

"Would you care to measure your strength against mine, human?" he sneered.

"Why not, indeed?" said the Soldier, taking his pipe from his mouth and rising slowly to his feet. "Can you squeeze water out of a stone?"

The eldest devil ordered some stones to be brought up from the street, and a small devil was soon back with a handful. He gave one to the old devil and one to the Soldier.

"You try first," said the Soldier.

The demon squeezed the stone so hard that it crumbled to dust.

"See that, human?" he exclaimed triumphantly.

The Soldier shrugged his shoulders contemptuously and took the large boiled beetroot out of his knapsack.

---

4. **veritable** not being false or imaginary
5. **bedlam** scene of confusion

"This stone is far larger than those pebbles you brought up," he said. "Now look!"

He squeezed the beetroot lightly between his hands until the juice began to drip from it like drops of blood. The devils looked at one another in silent amazement. After an embarrassed pause in which only the sound of the Soldier's jaws was audible, they asked him what he was chewing.

"Walnuts," replied the Soldier. "But none of you will be able to chew these walnuts of mine."

"Give me one and I'll try," said the old devil.

Instead of a walnut, however, the Soldier threw him over a bullet from his rifle. The devil popped the leaden bullet into his mouth and chewed and chewed with all the strength of his jaws, but could not crush it between his teeth. The Soldier continued to put one walnut after another into his mouth and, of course, to chew them up quite easily.

The devils were confused and ashamed.

"Well," said the Soldier, "you don't appear to be very good at eating my walnuts, but I always heard that the likes of you were good at assuming all manner of shapes and sizes. I have been told that big devils can become little ones, and little devils big ones, and that you can squeeze yourselves into any crack or crevice."

"So we can!" cried the devils in unison.

"I don't believe it!" said the Soldier, shaking his head. "I wager you cannot all squeeze yourselves into my old knapsack."

With that the demons rushed helter-skelter into the Soldier's knapsack, exulting[6] at the chance to prove their superiority, and within seconds there was not one of them left anywhere in the whole house. When the last hairy tail disappeared into the knapsack, the Soldier strolled over, shut it up tight and strapped and buckled it firmly.

"Now perhaps we'll have some peace and quiet," he muttered, and taking his overcoat off the hook, he wrapped himself up warm and slept soundly all night long.

The next morning the merchant sent two of his servants to find out whether the Soldier was still alive and in case he had perished at the hands of the demons, to bring back his bones. When they arrived, however, they found the Soldier wide awake and strolling round the room sucking his pipe.

"Good morning, Soldier," they said. "We certainly did not expect to find you among the living. Look, this box was for your bones!"

The Soldier laughed.

"It's a little early to think of burying me, I fear," he said. "But you can help me carry this knapsack to the blacksmith, if you like."

---

6. exulting rejoicing

They took the knapsack and carried it off to the smithy.

"Now, lads," said the Soldier to the blacksmith and his mates. "Put this bag on the anvil and hammer it flat for me."

The blacksmith placed the bag on the anvil and all three of them beat on it with their heavy hammers until the sweat ran down their brows and the whole village resounded to their blows.

"Help! Help!" screamed the tormented demons. "Soldier, have mercy! Let us out! Help!"

But the Soldier took no notice.

"Come on, lads," he said to the smiths. "Put some strength behind those blows! We have got to teach the likes of them not to take liberties with the likes of us!"

"Help! Mercy!" squealed the devils. "We promise never to come near the town again, let alone the merchant's house, and we will give you a king's ransom if you will only spare our lives!"

"Very well," said the Soldier. "But remember! don't ever try any of your tricks on a Russian soldier again!"

He ordered the blacksmiths to cease hammering at the sack, undid the straps and buckles and let the demons out one by one until only their leader remained inside.

"First bring me his ransom," said the Soldier, "and then I shall release him also."

Hardly had he time to light up his pipe than he saw a tiny devil approaching him carrying a leather bag.

"Here is the ransom," squeaked the devil.

The Soldier took the bag and was surprised to feel that it was so light. He unfolded it, looked inside, shook it, turned it inside out, held it up to the sun, but still he could find nothing in it.

"Now that you have had your little joke," he said, "I shall let your chief feel the taste of the hammers all by himself!"

The old devil in the knapsack gave a terrified squeal.

"No! don't hit me, Soldier!" he cried. "Listen! The bag is no ordinary bag. It is a magic one, and there is only one like it in the whole world. Make a wish, open the wallet and you will find that your wish has been fulfilled. If you want to capture anything or anybody, all you have to do is to open the bag, shake it and say 'Come on in!' and no one addressed in this way will be able to resist."

"I'll try it out to make sure it works all right," said the Soldier, and thought to himself: "What we could do with just now is three good bottles of beer."

Immediately the bag felt heavy, and when the Soldier opened it he found three bottles of beer inside. He handed them round to the blacksmith and his mates, proposed their health, and walked outside the smithy. He looked about him this way and that, and spying a sparrow perched on a rooftop he opened the bag and shook it in front of him.

"Come on in!" he said to the sparrow, and hardly had the words left his lips than the sparrow flew down from the rooftop straight into the magic bag.

"Well, it works all right," said the Soldier, "and no doubt it will prove quite useful."

And he went back into the forge and released the devil from his knapsack.

"But have a care," he warned him grimly. "If ever I set eyes on you or your brood again, I'll have you in this bag in a jiffy. And then look out for yourself!"

The devil ran off as fast as his legs would take him, his tail between his legs, and the Soldier went to the merchant.

"It's all clear now," he said. "You can move into your new house whenever you like."

When the merchant saw the Soldier standing before him with his servants, his jaw dropped in amazement and he could hardly believe his eyes.

"By Heaven, what you said about the Russian soldier is right enough!" he cried. "Water will not drown him nor fire burn him! How did you manage to get the better of the devils and come off scot-free?"

The Soldier told him all that had happened during the night and how he had got rid of the devils for ever. The merchant's servants corroborated[7] what he said, but the merchant thought it better to play for safety and to wait a while longer before moving into the house. In the evening, therefore, he sent his two servants to spend the night in the new house with the Soldier.

"Be on your guard," he told them, "and if anything happens, the Soldier will look after you."

Nothing did happen, however, and they all passed a quiet and peaceful night in the house and returned safe and sound to their master the following morning.

The third night the merchant himself decided to sleep in the house, and again the night passed without incident. The merchant was overjoyed at his good fortune, and the next morning he ordered all his possessions to be transferred to his new house and a great banquet to be prepared. Everything of the best was cooked and boiled and roasted and baked, wine flowed in profusion and the tables creaked under the strain. The Soldier was given the place of honour at the head of the table and all the many guests ate and drank to their heart's desire.

"Eat, drink, and enjoy yourself, Soldier," cried the host, "for I shall never forget your services as long as I live!"

---

7. **corroborated** confirmed

The merry company feasted until the early hours of the morning. When they finally broke up, the sun was already shining in at the window, and the Soldier hoisted his knapsack on his shoulder and prepared for the road.

The merchant was dismayed.

"What is the hurry, my good fellow?" he cried. "Stay with us and be our guest for a week, or a month, or as long as you like!"

"I thank you for your kind offer, merchant," replied the Soldier, "but I must go home to see my parents. I was only too glad to be of assistance to you."

The merchant opened his money-coffers and was about to fill the Soldier's knapsack with silver coins. The Soldier declined politely.

"You are very kind, merchant," he said, "but I have no use for silver. I still know a trick or two and shall no doubt get on all right by myself."

And taking his leave of the merchant, he stuffed his magic pouch into his knapsack and marched boldly out into the world. For a long way or for a little way he marched on until he came to a hill, and when he had climbed to the brow of the hill and looked down and saw the village where he was born nestling in the valley below, his heart was filled with joy and his soul felt as light as a feather. He quickened his pace and marched eagerly down the hill-side, gazing all the time around him at the budding trees, the silver lakes, the green hills, and the golden sun and sighing with happiness and pride.

"How beautiful you are, my Russian land," he murmured. "Many are the lands I know, and rich and wonderful are their towns, but none in the whole white world is as fair as you!"

And he walked joyously up to the little hut where he was born and knocked on the door. A bent old woman appeared on the threshold and the Soldier threw himself into her arms.

"My son, my son," cried the old woman. "We had long since given you up for dead. Your father longed to give you his blessing before he died, but alas! it is five years since he passed away with his wish unfulfilled."

The Soldier's old mother began to weep, but he kissed her cheek and hugged her and told her that she would never have to worry any more.

"Don't fret, matushka," he said softly. "Now that I am here I shall look after you."

He undid his pouch, thought of all manner of good things to eat and drink, and the magic pouch grew fat and bulky. The Soldier emptied it on the table.

"Eat and drink to your heart's content, matushka," he said, but the old woman was so overcome with emotion that she could scarcely touch a thing. But for all that she was very happy.

The next day the Soldier again undid the magic pouch, wished for some silver, and began to put the affairs of the farm in order. He built a new cottage, bought a cow and pigs and sheep in the market-place, and within a few weeks he had become one of the most prosperous farmers in the province. Then he found himself a bride, married and had children, and his old mother, whose happiness knew no bounds, looked after her grandchildren with great care.

For a long time they lived in perfect peace and happiness, but when six or seven years had passed, the Soldier suddenly fell ill. One day went by, then another, then a third, and still he could not rise from his bed and eat and drink. He grew weaker and weaker and then, on the eve of the fourth day, opening his eyes, which felt as heavy as lead, he saw that someone was standing at his bedside. It was a white skeleton! Slowly and deliberately the horrible vision whetted its great scythe[8] and stared grimly at the sick man. It was Death!

"I've come for you, Soldier," he said. "Get ready!"

"Wait a little longer, Death!" protested the Soldier. "There's still a good thirty years left in me! I've got to raise my children and marry them off. Come and see me again when I've done that, for I have no time to die at present."

"There's no leave in *my* Army, Soldier," chuckled Death, his bones rattling drily. "You won't get thirty years or thirty minutes from me."

"If you won't give me thirty years, Death," pleaded the Soldier, "give me three years' grace! You know I've a lot to do."

"Not three years nor three minutes!" exclaimed Death, impatiently sharpening his scythe. "You've got your marching orders, so jump to it!"

"*You* jump to it!" said the Soldier, and summoning up all his strength he pulled his magic pouch from beneath his pillow and waved it with a feeble hand. "Come in here!"

Scarcely had the words left the Soldier's lips than Death became a struggling bag of bones. The Soldier felt as though a heavy weight had lifted from his chest and he knew that he was better. He fastened the pouch securely, got up, sat at the table and ate a substantial meal of wholesome black bread, white cheese, and brown beer. When he finally pushed back his plate he felt as strong as ever, and sauntering up to the magic pouch he said:

"Well, Bony, you were not very civil to me, were you? That will teach you not to try to pull a fast one on a Russian soldier!"

A small, thin voice emerged from the depths of the bag.

"What are you going to do with me, Soldier?" asked Death.

"Well, I did not really want to lose a good pouch," said the Soldier gravely, "but there is nothing for it. I am going to drop you into the swamp and push you well down into the mud. You won't get up to any of your mischief there, I'll be bound!"

---

8. **scythe** tool used for cutting grass

"Let me out, Soldier!" squeaked Death. "I'll give you three years' grace!"

"What do you take me for? I've got you now, and I intend to keep you!"

"Let me out. I'll make it thirty years!"

The Soldier rubbed his hand thoughtfully over his stubbly chin.

"That's more like it," he said. "But if I let you out, you must promise me not to meddle with people's lives for thirty years, so that no one shall die in all that time."

"Soldier, I cannot promise that! What shall I live on?"

"You can eat roots and radishes in the fields."

Death made no answer, and the Soldier pulled on his boots.

"Have it your own way, Death," he said. "Hold tight, we're off to the swamp!"

He swung the bag roughly over his shoulder.

"Stop!" cried Death. "You win, Soldier. Let me go and I promise to live on roots and radishes and not to kill anyone for thirty years!"

A stifled sob sounded from the depths of the bag.

"All right, then!" said the Soldier. "But no treachery, mind! Keep your promise!"

With that he let Death out of the bag. Death jumped out, straightened his bones, picked up his scythe, and rattled off into the wood as fast as his legs would carry him. There he fell to eating roots and radishes. The Soldier's good flesh would have been better, but alas! there was nothing to be done.

And so the Soldier lived happily on with his mother and wife and children with never a thought for Death. One day, however, when he was busy sowing in the fields, he felt a sudden tap on his shoulder, and with some surprise saw the grinning skull of Death beside him.

"Your thirty years are up, Soldier," he said. "Are you ready?"

"Ah, well!" said the Soldier, shrugging his shoulders. "A deal's a deal, and discipline's discipline. If my time is up, bring me my coffin."

Death required no second bidding. He gleefully dragged up a large coffin with wrought-iron clasps and raised the lid.

"Hop in, Soldier!" he said.

The Soldier's face flushed in anger.

"Hop in? *Hop in?*" he exclaimed. "How do you think I know the drill for getting into a coffin? I am an old soldier. You show me the movements and I'll perform the manœuvre in correct order."

"Very well, Soldier," said Death. "One might as well die as one has lived. I'll show you what to do." He laid himself carefully into the coffin. "Look, it's easy. Just lie down naturally, so. Stretch out your legs, so. Then cross your hands at right angles on your chest, so. One, two, three, so!"

The Soldier, however, had always been better on the battlefield than the parade-ground, and as soon as Death was comfortably settled in the coffin, he slammed down the lid, banged in the nails, loaded it on to a cart, and drove it off to the river.

"You go, Death!" he chuckled. "I don't think I shall volunteer after all."

With a great splash, the heavy oak coffin fell into the river, and the swift stream bore it rapidly out to sea, where for many years Death floated helplessly around on the choppy waves.

When some years had passed, however, and Death's bones were beginning to turn a little green, and seaweed and barnacles covered the coffin, a severe storm blew up, huge waves dashed against its sides and finally swept it hard against the rocks on the seashore. The wood splintered and shattered, and Death, more dead than alive, flopped wearily on to the beach like a stringless marionette.[9] He rested there for several hours, cleaning his rusty scythe and muttering to himself, and then rose to his feet and set out in search of the wily[10] old Russian soldier. By now he had learned to be cautious in his dealings with him, and when he came to his farm, he cunningly hid in a corner and waited patiently for him to pass by.

The Soldier was preparing to go and sow the corn at the time, and he was just going into the granary with an empty sack to fill with seeds when Death darted out from behind the door and stood before him.

"Got you!" he cried. "Surrender, Soldier, for you won't get away now!"

"I'm in a tight corner here!" thought the Soldier, but taking his empty and harmless corn sack from his breast, he waved it threateningly in Death's grinning face.

"So you're back again, are you?" he cried. "I take it you want to spend a holiday in my sack at the bottom of the swamp?"

As soon as Death saw the empty corn sack waving in his face, he took it to be the Soldier's magic pouch, and though the grin could not exactly disappear from his fleshless face, he turned as pale as death is usually thought to be, and before the Soldier could say another word, he took to his heels and fled, if one may use the expression in his case, for dear life.

And thus it was, they say, that the Soldier was the very last person ever to see Death clearly in front of his eyes, for since that day Death always creeps up on people unseen and invisible. His one preoccupation is not to be seen by the Soldier, for there is nothing he dreads so much as spending eternity at the bottom of the slimy green swamp. And the Soldier lived happily ever after, and even now he is still alive and kicking.

That, at least, is how some say the story ended, but there are others who intimate that the Soldier's victory over Death was not so clever, after all,

---

9. **marionette** wooden doll with jointed limbs moved by wires

10. **wily** crafty

and had quite serious consequences for himself and his fellow men. These people say that when the Soldier first trapped Death in his bag he did not release him again in exchange for any promise, but took him into the dark Brianski Wood, hung him on the top of a trembling aspen-tree, and returned home intending to get on with his work unimpaired by the importunity[11] of this wearisome fellow Death. And from that day on, although baby after baby was born as regularly as before, no one in the whole white world died at all.

Many years passed by and the Soldier had all but forgotten about poor Death hanging up in a bag on the top of a tree, when one day, on his way to town, he met an old, old woman coming along the road in the opposite direction, and the old woman was so weak and frail and her great years weighed so heavily upon her poor bony shoulders that she blew from side to side at the slightest gust of wind.

"Lord! What an old woman that is, to be sure!" said the Soldier. "She ought to have been dead long ago, poor old soul!"

"You are right, Soldier," quavered the old woman. "I ought to have been dead long ago. When you tricked Death to enter your bag these many years ago, I had but one more hour to live. I should be glad to go to my rest, Soldier, for Death is merciful to such as me. Beware, Soldier, for the day will come when you too will suffer what you have inflicted on me!"

With this, the old woman went her way and left the Soldier deep in thought.

"The Russian proverb says that old age is no joy but death is no gain," he thought to himself. "But the old woman is right. I have already many sins against my name and am already pretty old. It is better to die now and avoid the torments of a decrepit old age unworthy of a soldier. And the older I get, the more I'll suffer."

So the Soldier went to Brianski Wood and found the aspen-tree at the top of which the bag was rocking dizzily to and fro in the breeze.

"Are you still alive, Death?" called the Soldier.

"Only just, Soldier," faltered a weak and muffled voice from inside the sack.

The Soldier climbed the tree, took down the bag, and carried it home. Then he lay down on the bed, bade farewell to his wife and children, and opening the bag, asked Death to finish him off.

As soon as the bag was open, however, Death leapt to the floor, and out of the door in a flash, he made off as fast as his legs would carry him.

"Go to Hell and may the devil take you, Soldier!" he called back. "I never want to set eyes on you again!"

---

11. **importunity** excessively persistent urging

With that he was gone, and there was nothing for the Soldier to do but get up and get dressed, for he was as alive and well as ever. The thought that he would grow older and older and never die, however, began to prey on his mind, and in the end he decided to follow Death's parting advice and persuade the devils to take him.

"They will throw me into a cauldron of boiling pitch," he thought, "but in the end my sins will be washed away."

Taking once again his leave of his wife and children, he walked down to Hell with his magic pouch in his hand until he came to the grim sentinel at Hell's Gate.

"Who goes there?" challenged the devil.

"A sinner who has come to be tormented for his sins," replied the Soldier.

"Come in," said the devil. "We don't have many volunteers for our Army. Wait a minute, though! What is that in your hand?"

"A sack."

The sentinel took a sharp pace to the rear.

"Help! Sound the alarm!" he yelled.

The devils scurried to and fro and within seconds the Gates of Hell were barred and bolted and the windows shuttered. The Soldier scratched his head, for he had not expected this unfriendly reception, and walking round the walls he called out to the Prince of the Devils.

"Let me into Hell, Beelzebub!" he cried. "I have come to be tormented for my sins."

"There's no room here for you," said Beelzebub. "It wouldn't be long before we were all struggling and suffocating in that blessed bag of yours!"

"Very well," said the Soldier. "If you won't let me in, at least give me two hundred souls that I might lead them to Heaven. Perhaps God will forgive me my sins for this deed."

"You can have two hundred and fifty souls," cried Beelzebub, "but go away from here!"

The Prince of Hell ordered two hundred and fifty souls to be let out at the back so that the Soldier should not somehow slip inside, and the Soldier formed up his platoon in fours and marched them off to Paradise.

When the Apostles saw the band approaching, they informed the Lord and asked for His instructions.

"Let the two hundred and fifty souls pass through the Gates of Heaven," said God. "But for goodness sake don't let the Soldier in, or he'll have us all inside that infernal bag of his before long."

When he heard this bad news, the Soldier took one of the souls aside, and giving him his magic pouch, he whispered:

"Once you're inside the Heavenly Gates, just open the bag and say aloud: 'Soldier, jump in here!'"

The soul took the bag, the Heavenly Gates opened, and the two hundred and fifty souls marched in. Such was their joy upon entering Heaven, however, that the soul forgot all about the Soldier and his bag, and after waiting a long time in vain outside the walls of Paradise, the Soldier resigned himself to his fate and walked sadly away to wander unhappily about the wide, white world for all eternity, unwanted and unwelcome in every place.

And only the other day, they say, did he finally die.

Anna Akhmatova | Requiem[1]

Like Aleksandr Solzhenitsyn, Anna Akhmatova did not escape the brutality of the dictator Joseph Stalin. Her son was imprisoned as a political enemy, and she was not allowed to publish her poetry or travel outside Russia. This poem was inspired by the sight of others like herself waiting at a prison gate for some word of imprisoned family members.

IN THE TERRIBLE YEARS of the Yezhov period I spent seventeen months waiting in line outside Leningrad's prisons. On one occasion, someone "recognized" me. Then the woman behind me, her lips blue with cold, who, of course, had never heard of me, emerged from the stupor which held us all and whispered (we all whispered then) this question in my ear:

"Could you describe this?"

And I said: "I could."

Then something like a smile passed over what had once been her face.

1

At dawn they came for you.
I trailed behind—it was like
A funeral. In the darkened room
Children cried. The icon candle died.
The icon had left its coldness on your lips,
And oh, the deathly film of sweat upon your brow!
Like the wives of those who mutinied[2] against the tsar,[3]
Under the Kremlin's towers I shall howl.

1935

---

1. **requiem** a solemn chant for the dead
2. **mutinied** rebelled against a lawful authority
3. **tsar** ruler of Russia

2

Quietly flows the quiet Don,
The housebreaking yellow moon

Enters with its hat askew.
A shadow greets the yellow moon.

Whose shadow? See, it is a woman,
A woman ailing and alone.

Dead is her husband, gaol[4] claims her son,
Pray for me, everyone.

3

No, it is not I, it is another who suffers.
I could not have borne such suffering; let what has happened
Be draped in black cloth.
And away with lamps . . .
                              Night.

4

They should have shown you, little scoffer,
Apple of everyone's eye,
Delinquent of Tsarskoye Selo,
What your life was going to be like,
How you would stand before
The prison, three-hundredth in line,
Clasping a parcel, your tears
Scalding the New Year's ice.
The prison poplar is swaying.
In the soundlessness, we ask how many
Innocent lives will be taken . . . .

5

For seventeen months I have cried out,
Ceaselessly I call
You home. My son, you are my nightmare now—
At the executioner's feet I fall.
Everywhere is confusion.

---

4. **gaol** jail

How can I tell apart
Man the beast and man the human?—
And how soon is the sentence to be carried out?
Only dusty flowers are left,
A tinkling censer, tracks
Somewhere—leading nowhere;
And looking me straight in the eye,
A menacing presage[5] of death,
This enormous star.

6

Weeks fleetly run on.
I can't believe it happened:
How the white nights[6] saw
Into your cell, my son;
And how what they now see,
With burning hawk-like eye,
Of your tall cross, they tell—
And of your agony.
                    1939

7 The Sentence

And the stone word
Struck my still living breast.
No matter—I was prepared.
Somehow I shall last.

Today there is much to be done.
I must kill off memory,
My heart must be changed into stone,
I must learn to live again.

Or else. . . . Hot summer rustles
Festively outside my window.
Long ago I had a premonition
Of this bright day, this empty house.
                    Summer 1939

---

5. **presage** warning or indication of the future
6. **white nights** midsummer season when it is daylight almost 24 hours a day

8 To Death

You'll come anyway—so, why not now?
I am expecting you—life is an ordeal.
I've put out the light and opened the door
For you, so simple, so wonderful.
Take any form you like for this,
A shellburst leaking poison,
Or like a seasoned criminal, neatly dispatch me,
Or poison me with typhoid fumes,
Or, as in that tale you dreamt up,
So sickeningly familiar to all,
The top of your blue cap
Peeking behind the palefaced janitor.
I don't care anymore. The Yenisey
Swirls, the North Star shines.
And an ultimate horror overlays
The blueness of my dear one's eyes.

> *19 August 1939*
> *The House on the Fontanka*
> *Leningrad*

9

Already madness has taken
Half my soul under its wing,
Giving me heady wine to drink,
Into a dark valley beckoning.

And I have come to terms with this:
The battle's lost. I listen to
My ravings, and it seems as if
They come from some place far removed.

And it is not permitted me
To take away anything. Although
I importune madness with my pleas—
The answer's always 'No.'

Not my son's agonized look,
His suffering wrought in stone,
Nor that day the storm broke,
Nor the visiting hour in prison,

Nor the cool feel of your hands,
The agitated shadows of the lime trees,
Nor the faint distant sounds,
The last few words consoling me.
4 May 1940
The House on the Fontanka

10 Crucifixion

"Weep not for me, Mother,
I am in my grave."

I
A choir of angels hymned the hour,
The heavens were on fire, and he
Said, "Why have You forsaken me, oh Father?"
And, "Mother, weep not for me."

II
Sobbing, Mary Magdelene writhed,
His favorite disciple stiffened,
And no one even dared to cast his eye
Upon the Mother, standing silent.
1940–1943

Epilogue

I
I learnt how faces crumple, how fear
Gazes from under eyelids, how
Suffering's hard cuneiform[7]
Is etched on cheek and brow;
How black or ashen locks turn
In moments, not in years, to white,
How the smile fades on uncomplaining lips
And dry fearful laughter vibrates.
I pray not for myself alone,
But for those who stood with me, for all
Who in July heat or cruel cold
Stood by the blinded red-brick wall.

---

7. **cuneiform** wedge-shaped characters used in writing

II
Again the dead hour has come, I remember
The dead: I feel, I cry, I hear:

The one who could scarcely be led to her end,
The one who no more trod her native land,

The one who tossed her beautiful head:
"I come here as if to my home," she said.

I should like to recall each one by name
But cannot—the list has been taken away,

And so, instead, I have woven a shroud
Out of their poor words overheard.

I remember them always and everywhere,
I shall not forget, beset by new cares.

And if my tormented mouth is shut,
My mouth, through which millions cry out,

Let them likewise remember me
On the eve of my memorial day.

And if some day in this country it's thought
To raise a memorial in my honor,

I'll give my consent to this accolade—
But on one condition: let it not be raised

Either by that sea where I was born—
The last link with that sea has been broken—

Or in the park at Tsarskoye, close
By the cherished tree stump with its stricken shadow,

But here, where I've stood three hundred hours
And where they never unbolted the doors.

For even in blessed death I fear
To forget the rumble of Black Marias,

Forget how that vile door slammed in the face
Of the old woman howling like a wounded beast.

So let the snow flow down like tears
From my bronzen eyelids motionless,

And let the distant call of the prison dove
Boom, and silent boats sail the Neva.[8]

March 1940

---

8. **Neva** river flowing through St. Petersburg (then Leningrad) into the Gulf of Finland

Nat Hentoff

Bringing the First Amendment (Live!) into the Schools

from
Free Speech for Me—
But Not for Thee:
How the American Left
and Right Relentlessly
Censor Each Other

The First Amendment to the United States Constitution guarantees the right of all citizens to express their opinions on public matters, even when they disagree with official policy and actions. Nat Hentoff, a frequent commentator on First Amendment issues, fears that too few Americans appreciate our constitutional right to disagree.

IN HIS FAREWELL ADDRESS to the American people, Ronald Reagan said, "If we forget what we did, we won't know who we are. I am warning of an eradication . . . of the American memory that could result, ultimately, in an erosion of the American spirit."

That erosion is already taking place, particularly among schoolchildren. Every year for the past quarter century, I have been spending a fair amount of time as a guest speaker in high schools, junior high schools, and some elementary schools around the country—from rural classrooms in Pennsylvania to big, fast-track high schools in Colorado. I've been in most of the states, and from time to time I also talk with students from various cities on radio call-in shows.

Most American kids are ignorant of their history as a free people. They know very little of what's in the Bill of Rights and the Fourteenth Amendment, and they know less of what it took to secure these liberties and rights. And if they leave school with such ignorance, they are hardly likely, as adults, to fight to preserve their own liberties—let alone anyone else's. The young have not forgotten what Americans have done. They have simply never known.

For instance, not long ago at a middle school near Harrisburg, Pennsylvania, we were talking about the extent—and limitations—of the power of the police. I asked the students what they knew about the Fourth Amendment. Heavy silence. Finally, a brave youngster informed me that the Fourth Amendment was about the right to bear arms.

"Okay," I said, "let me tell you the story of the Fourth Amendment." (When I once told Supreme Court Justice William Brennan that I occasionally try to bring the words of the Constitution off the page and into the inner thoughts of the young, he said, "Tell them stories! Tell them stories!" And I always do.)

That morning, I told the future voters—and maybe some of the future legislators—of Pennsylvania about the writs of assistance (the general search warrants) that British SWAT teams used as they smashed into colonists' homes and turned everything upside down, including the colonists, to pry into cupboards and under beds for goods on which taxes had not been paid. These were random searches. The British troops did not need to have any reason to believe there was contraband in the home. They battered their way in when and wherever they pleased.

The faces before me grew indignant. I told them of fiery James Otis arguing long and fiercely against those writs in a Massachusetts court in 1761. And I told them of a young lawyer, John Adams, watching spellbound in that courtroom and then writing later that "the independence was then and there born."

The kids thought that was a neat story. They wanted to know more. They always do. I have yet to be in a classroom where—once the Constitution becomes inhabited by actual people—students are not eager to search further into that suddenly compelling document. Some of them look as though they've just discovered America.

In a few schools, I have found kids to whom the Constitution had already become something personal. That is, they actually felt it belonged to them. And some had used "the living Constitution" as an Excalibur[1] against their principal or school board. Invariably, these students had come to their familiarity with the Constitution because a teacher had made those rights and liberties stay in their minds long after classes were over. . . .

---

1. **Excalibur** King Arthur's sword

But there are times when what at first appears to be a potentially disruptive school experience can turn into what Oliver Wendell Holmes once described as the core of our system of free expression:

"If there is any principle of the Constitution that more imperatively calls for attachment than any other, it is the principle of free thought—not free thought for those who agree with us, but freedom for the thought we hate."

Belief in this principle hardly comes naturally, and it has not been learned by the vast majority of American adults or by their children. But it *can* be taught, as was demonstrated in 1988 at the North Garner Middle School in a town near Raleigh, North Carolina.

One morning, Mark Vice, Jr., a ninth-grader, came to school wearing a Confederate flag sewn onto the back of his denim jacket. The flag had been a Christmas present from his father, who has a Confederate flag tattooed on his forearm. The school's principal, Dr. Janet Stevens, who had asked Mark not to wear the jacket in school, forbade him to enter if he persisted.

Mark's parents went for help to the North Carolina Civil Liberties Union. ("These are his rights they're messing with," his father said.) One of its attorneys, William Simpson, together with the school's principal and the superintendent of schools, agreed that rather than get into a court battle, they would hold an assembly and let the kids hear the conflicting points of view. About 30 percent of the 850 students are black, and many had bristled at the sight of the jacket. There had been black-white tensions, including fisticuffs,[2] at the school before.

A number of people spoke at the assembly, but Simpson's talk made the most lasting impression on the students. He told them that "today the Confederate flag is not very popular with school officials. Twenty years ago, the symbols of the civil rights movement were not very popular with many school officials.

"In the 1960s, black people marched in all parts of the South to bring down legalized racism. . . . Everywhere they marched they offended many white people who believed things were fine just the way they were. Those marchers faced angry white crowds who were disturbed by the marchers' message. If the hostile reaction of those crowds had justified bans on demonstrations and marches, there would be no Civil Rights Act or Voting Rights Act or integrated restaurants and motels.

"Instead of going to school and working together, black and white people would be at odds—much like they are today in South Africa, where for so long there was no freedom of speech."

In addition to the assembly, the principal had debates in each classroom,

---

2. **fisticuffs** fighting with fists

and then in a schoolwide meeting of representatives of each classroom, on whether hateful speech should be protected. Out of all this robust exchange of views throughout the school, there came an understanding on the part of most of the kids—from hearing viewpoints other than their own—that maybe this free-speech thing should apply to everybody. Mark Vice, Jr., came back to school, the Confederate flag still stitched to his jacket, and there were no disruptions—even though about a dozen other students started wearing Confederate flags to school.

(Originally, the North Carolina Civil Liberties Union had said in taking the case: "Even though we as an organization do not agree with the values represented by the symbol, he has the right to wear the symbol so long as he is not disrupting the educational process.")

Dr. Janet Stevens made a point of telling me: "I lifted the ban without Mark or anyone else knowing I was going to do it. I didn't want any group, including the ACLU, to think they can control this school."

Summing up the testing at the North Garner Middle School of Oliver Wendell Holmes's definition of true free speech, Dr. Stevens said: "Well, there was a real exchange of ideas. For the first time, they, black and white, have heard each other—however reluctantly."

From the beginning, the *Raleigh News and Observer*, a much respected newspaper, had become involved in the dispute. In an editorial, the paper quoted, with ringing approval, from the Supreme Court's 1969 *Tinker* decision:

"Undifferentiated fear or apprehension of disturbance is not enough to overcome the right to freedom of expression. . . . It can hardly be argued that either students or teachers shed their constitutional rights to freedom of speech at the schoolhouse gate. . . ." . . .